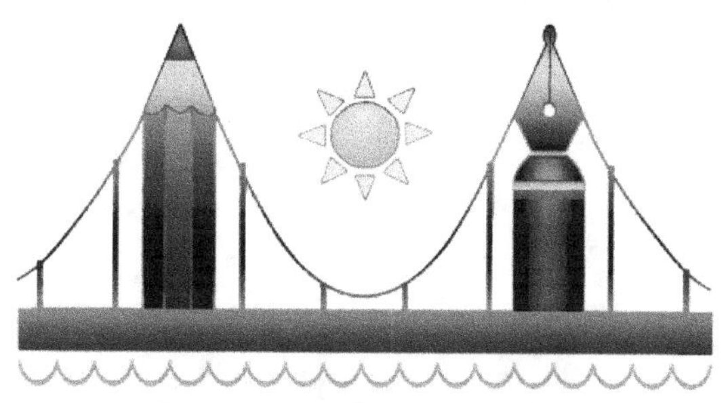

SAN FRANCISCO WRITERS CONFERENCE

Learn. Connect. Publish.

2024 Writing Contest Anthology

HOW WE CHANGE

First Edition

Designed and Produced by Lissa Provost at
New Alexandria Creative Group
For the San Francisco Writers Foundation

©Copyright 2024 by the San Francisco Writers Foundation
All rights reserved by the individual authors.

www.NewAlexandriaCG.com
www.SFWriters.org
Available everywhere via print on demand.
Please support your local bookstores.
Print ISBN: 978-1-64715-011-2
eBook ISBN: 978-1-64715-012-9

Dear Reader,

It is our privilege once again to introduce you to a remarkable slate of rising authors and poets by way of this, our fourth anthology of Writing Contest Winner and Finalist entries. Because we don't wrap this contest around a theme, we look for one to emerge as we edit together the entries that impressed us. It's not always easy to find a common thread between work in diverse genres, but it's always interesting as it feels revelatory about how we're experiencing aspects of life in common. The thread of our beliefs emerged last year, and the ways they shift as we navigate life inspired the Lombard Street photo on the cover. It seemed appropriate for a theme of general reflection to follow the sensory-intense post-lockdown anthology. But what comes next?

The conference has, through most of its history, held a Writing for Change one-day conference. In recent years, this has become a track within the main conference. When we asked the question in a general session of the conference "who here is motivated to write by a desire to change the world for the better?" the vast majority of attendees raised their hands.

Change, and narratives illustrating personal change in particular, dominate this anthology. From the adventurous protagonist of **GADIA**, our winning KidLit entry, suddenly seeing a familiar sight differently in a way that sets him on a new course, the bullied kid finally fighting back in the runner-up, ***Guys Like Us***, to both Historical and Futuristic protagonists in Adult Fiction like our category winner, ***Island of Machines***, to the intense honesty and openness in Adult Nonfiction like **On Dating & Job Searching**, even in Poetry, the theme of *How We Change* kept catching in our minds. What we write is a model for how life was, is, or can be, and Writing for Change in fiction is often about being deliberate with how it can be, and in nonfiction about how it was and now is. It's about modeling the change we want to see in the world.

We write in different ways, but we're all coming to terms with the new world that has emerged. Perhaps not every entry is a perfect fit for this idea, but I think all of us are keen to help those around us learn from the past, and envision a better future. We are modeling for the world we want to see. We are writing for change by showing examples of how our characters change. We were captivated again and again, and cannot wait to read more.

CONGRATULATIONS! To all our finalists and winners. We look forward to meeting many of you at the conference and will watch your careers with great interest.

Sincerely,

The San Francisco Writers Conference Executive Board

Find out more about the San Francisco Writers Conference, including our next writing contest, at SFWriters.org.

Contents

Children's and Young Adult

Grand Prize Winner
GADIA
by Su Mon Han

Prologue

Gadia
Be it with my final breath, I will reach you.
The last place in the world undiscovered;
Your glory shall be mine someday.
For I know in my heart that you bide there unbreachable
Waiting only for me to breach.

It will be me, I hiss to my coiling doubts, I will be the one.
Let it be me, I call in prayer to the clouds, let me be the one.
And let it be the one, I beseech it, the last place I set my feet upon.

Let it be now, then, before my dreams and bones turn to dust.
Let it be Gadia.

— "Invocation," *The Eperium*, Phidarus the Poet (108 G.A.)

For the last 499 years, the floating continent of Gadia has hovered unmoving in the eastern sky, a dark smudge against the blazing dawn horizon. Most days, only the three topmost tips of its rocky skyline are visible out of the swath of clouds surrounding it perpetually; these clouds move in their own mysterious patterns, unmindful of the trade winds sweeping the skies around them.

The entire island appears that way: there, but not; existing, but detached; churning the blue waters beneath it for miles around but casting no shadow upon them. Like a fragment punched out of another landscape and laid upon the world's canvas, there it abides, massive and elusive, for all those along the distant shores to see.

Calystel was not amongst those fortunate enough to live in the prosperous port towns along Sorannia's mild coast, but he saw Gadia on a daily basis nonetheless.

He saw the island in his dreams.

Which is not to say in any figurative sense that the boy dreamed, like so many, of being the one to finally unlock the ancient puzzles and powerful barrier spells that guarded the floating isle; in the case of our Calystel, the dreams of Gadia he had were actual, literal dreams—a self-same one that had plagued him every night for nearly all of his young life.

In it, he stood upon a supremely tall and solitary peak of pale, luminous rock. It was joined at its distant base to the range of rocky hills encircling it, but these others stood a ways back from Calystel's peak and barely reached its half in height. It was almost a scene of kneeling retainers prostrating themselves at a respectful distance from their liege lord—or so Calystel had mused once or twice in the copious time he had spent there.

Perhaps he stood there for hours each night, for every minute his physical self spent in slumber; perhaps it was but the last, fleeting seconds of a dreamless sleep that stretched only in his own mind to infinity. It made little difference to Calystel; the time he spent alone with the howling wind and empty sky felt as real and abundant to him as his waking hours did, so long had he stood still upon that narrow peak, unable to descend or rest, or move or sit, or do much other than endure the brisk, cold winds that whipped around him.

Still, it had never occurred to him to try to escape that peak, to take the desperate if illusory plunge half a step in any direction. For to Calystel, despite his sufferings, the peak was not a place of imprisonment; it was his salvation, a last bastion of safety from what he knew lay seething and faceless below, waiting so very keenly for the day he would give in to his weariness and stumble from his keep.

It was the shadows.

There were always shadows on the edge of his dreams—though just the edge; they never appeared directly before him anymore. Still, he always knew, always felt them to be there, biding their time, watching eagerly, hungrily, to end their long-lived fast. Like the last, curling traces of chimney smoke dissolving into a frosty morning, they melted out of his field of vision wherever he turned—*just* as he turned—clearest out of the corners of his eyes.

They hadn't always stayed away. In his earliest memories, Calystel recalled the Dark, the endless nights of fear and running, hunted by that silent, surging, ominous mass. They were not like any nightmare creature he had ever dreamt before, and instinctively, he had known that the obliteration they intended for him was as real and absolute as a knife through the heart. He had been terrified to sleep, had screamed and cried and begged not to be taken to bed. But the adults hadn't understood.

"They're just dreams, you silly boy," they had said, and smiled tolerantly at his tantrums, wiped his tears, murmured comforting words as they tucked him in and then blew the candle out.

He had been on the verge of losing his mind, spending his nights fighting the sleep that his young body slipped so naturally into, pleading for help to increasingly deaf and obstinate ears. It was only then—when the last thread stretched on the verge of breaking—that salvation had come of its own accord.

Him; a man; someone Calystel didn't know, whose face he still did not know, for it had remained obscured in a brilliant light for all the time he had been there. In a blinding moment, his light had pushed away all the darkness and the snarling phantoms within it, created this glowing space, these peaks, this unending blue sky, and Calystel safely isolated on his island of stone.

"Who are you?" the boy had asked of the stranger, who had stood hovering in the air beside him.

"Grow strong, Calystel," the man had replied, and for a moment, the light from his tall wizards' staff had dimmed enough for the boy to catch sight of one eye—his left eye, vivid amidst his pale face and hair. Calystel couldn't tell its color, because there was a jagged rim of gold around the pupil that emitted its own startling light.

"If you want to find me, grow strong, Calystel," the man had said again and then turned his eyes up, toward something high above them.

When Calystel had turned to look as well, he had nearly stumbled off his narrow perch in surprise; for there floated the great island of Gadia, unshrouded and closer than any man had seen it in nearly 500 years. And from that day, he knew.

Gadia was his, and his father waited there for him.

Chapter 1: Those Who Hunt Shadows

Calystel woke groggily to the sound of his name being called.

"Calystel! Where *are* you?" an insistent voice cried, somewhere off to his right.

Somewhere you'll never find me, Calystel thought, and then turned over to find a more comfortable position in the cramped space. *Now go away and let me sleep a little more.*

The voice kindly obliged and Calystel had just managed to doze off again when he heard another voice—much closer this time—saying conspiratorially, "So tell me already, what was the *thing* in the jar?"

Don't you all have breakfast to eat? Calystel thought, and tried to block out the hushed conversation until something the intruder's companion said caught his attention.

"A Shadow," the second voice had whispered eagerly. "There's no doubt about it. It's how you transport them, in fact—in relicked containers called Sealing Jars. I was just reading about—"

"A real Shadow!" interrupted the first voice in an excited whisper. "Then that means the Paladin Cadets are up for their first combat test today!"

"Oh, yes; I have it from a *very* reliable source that it's happening right after lunch hour on the rear training grounds."

"No wonder the seniors all looked so tense at breakfast," said the other. "We have to go watch—I've never seen a real Shadow up close before!"

So much the better for you, thought Calystel, but pricked his ears up to attention anyhow.

"It's a weak one, of course," the second—slightly nasally—voice was saying. "They wouldn't start new Paladin Teams off with anything that could do any *real* damage."

"That's a shame," said the first voice. "If I were—" He cut off as the questing voice from earlier filled the hallway again, apparently returned from its circuit of the school. Calystel grimaced.

"Calystel!" it was calling again. Seeming to spot the two whisperers, it approached and asked, "Have either of you seen Cal this morning? He wasn't at breakfast and he's not in his room."

"Cal?" asked the first voice, which sounded familiar now that it wasn't speaking in a whisper. "If he's missing, that means he must be..."

Light suddenly flooded Calystel's vision as the door he had been leaning on opened from the outside. He tumbled unceremoniously to the floor.

"...right here!" Kenthas (the first voice) finished triumphantly.

"There you are!" cried Tinda, stamping her foot. "I've been looking everywhere for you, and you've been hiding in a *cupboard*?"

"Not hiding... exactly," Calystel muttered, though he had, in fact, scrambled into this secret napping spot at the first clank of an armored footstep that morning.

Su Mon Han has written countless resumés over the past fifteen years ending with the random tidbit: "Enjoys reading, baking, and singing karaoke; is also eternally writing her first novel." Happily, Su Mon can finally report that this prolonged and shambolic endeavor has concluded – Book One of her epic fantasy YA series GADIA is complete, and she is actively seeking representation (as well as one of those Cinderella story book deals – complete with Netflix option, of course – that every aspiring author lulls themself to sleep with each night...). You can find her daydreaming in this irresponsible fashion at DreamCompendium.com – please come and connect!

Category Winner
Guys Like Us
by Danielle Sunshine

News Headline

Newspaper clipping from the *Cincinnati Enquirer*, October 10, 1919

Cincinnati Reds – World's Champions 1919

"They have come through to victory. So hail to Pat Moran's bold and resourceful team of Cincinnati Reds, champions of the baseball world! With powerful bats and bright, keen eyes, with speed, agility and nerve, the champions of the National League tore through the defense of the White Sox this afternoon and clinched the world's honors..."

by Jack Ryder

September 25, 1920

Chapter 1: *Psssshshsh*...Smack-dab in the Eye

Solomon Skaletsky grinned as the wad of mud he'd scraped up from the bottom of the Ohio River hit Wolf Goldschmidt smack-dab in the eye. Sol wasn't a mean kid by any standards, but he could land a wad of river mud in anyone's eye if they deserved it bad enough. The way he saw it, standing in the muddy shallows as Wolf gloated down from the wooden dock, there wasn't a kid in Cincinnati who deserved it more.

It was all on account of what Wolf had said about the Reds—the Cincinnati Reds, that is—also known as the world's best baseball team. Wolf was mouthing off about how the Reds hadn't *really* won the World Series the previous October, even though everyone in the whole entire country knew they had.

"I'll get you good for this, Skaletsky," Wolf said, wiping the mud off his face, "Just as soon as you get out of the water."

Sol gazed at Wolf and stood up straighter. "Why don't you come in here and get me?"

Maury Jacobson, Sol's buddy who was doggy-paddling a few feet away, looked at him like he'd gone batty. "What kinda dumb idea is that?" he hissed.

It was a good question. Wolf was the biggest sixth grader in town and probably the meanest. Inviting him into the water was about as smart as asking a shark to come swimming. But Sol had a suspicion about Wolf and now was as good a time as any to test it.

Wolf stepped to the edge of the dock and stared hard into the river, clenching his fists like a prizefighter. A minute passed. Then two. Then three.

"I'll bet you my Eddie Roush 1919 Champions postcard he won't so much as dip his big toe in the water," Sol whispered. Maury held tight to the soggy rabbit's foot hanging around his neck.

Sol wasn't a big better, not like some kids who gambled away their pennies in street-corner craps games, but the facts pretty much spoke for themselves. Wolf had been coming around the Public Landing for years, pestering the little kids and stealing the clothes off the bigger ones, and in all that time, he'd never once gotten into the water. Even when the mercury topped a hundred degrees. Sol figured Wolf didn't know how to swim, and no amount of staring into the water was going to change that.

The minutes dragged on, and Sol grew more and more confident. Everything would be fine, just as long as he stayed in the water. "You gonna come in here and get me or aren't you?" he said, squinting into the sun.

Maury was breathing hard. He hated fighting more than any other kid Sol knew. Called himself a pacifist, whatever that was.

Wolf finally stepped forward, and something flickered in his eyes—something dark and mean. A second later he was swinging his arms, looking like he might jump in. Sol flinched, taking in a mouthful of water.

"Look at that. I ain't laid a finger on you and you're already drowning," Wolf said. "Just relax, Skaletsky, 'cause I'm not coming in after you. You're not worth it. But I ain't lying neither. The news about the fix is in all the papers. You'll see soon enough."

The fix.

It couldn't be true. It just couldn't be. The Reds had won the Series on the square. Sol had seen it with his own eyes, cutting school to climb onto the rooftops behind Redland Field, wedging his feet under the backside of the kid in front of him to keep from slipping down the shingles. He'd commemorated every hit and every run, including Dutch Ruether's glorious three bagger in the 4th inning of Game 1, on scorecards he'd mounted on his bedroom wall—a shrine to his beloved team. And now Wolf was saying the Chicago White Sox had lost on purpose. That they'd thrown the Series just to make a buck. It was enough to make a kid sick.

"Shut up, Wolf!" Sol slapped the water, and the sting on his palms worked itself all the way up his arm. "I saw Shoeless Joe hit a home run in the third inning of the final game. If that's not proof enough that the White Sox wanted to win, I don't know what is."

He hadn't really. Seen Shoeless Joe, that is. It cost too much money to travel all the way to Chicago on the train for the last game of the Series. And with tickets going for more than twenty-five dollars a-piece, well, only folks like Uncle Abram and rich kids like Wolf could afford to do stuff like that. Still, Sol wasn't going to back down. He knew for a fact that Shoeless Joe hit that homerun. It was in all the papers. And ball players who hit home runs wanted to win. Everybody knew that.

Wolf spat into the water. "I don't care what you saw, Skaletsky. What's true is true." He reached into his back pocket and pulled out a rolled-up newspaper. "It's all right here in black and white. The only reason the Reds took home the championship is because the Chicago White Sox let them win."

Sol clenched his teeth. He'd heard enough. He leaned down and gathered up more mud, packing it hard into a ball. A second later, it was flying through the air... *psssshshsh*...another one, smack-dab in the eye.

"Skaletsky!" Wolf waved his fist high in the air. "You good-for-nothing Bolshevik! You're dead. Deader than dead."

Good-for-nothing Bolshevik.

"You and your good-for-nothing family ought to go back to the old country where you belong."

Go back to the old country. Sol had heard some mean insults over the years, but... well, even Maury's mouth was hanging open in disbelief.

Everyone knew the Bolsheviks were un-American. Even Mrs. Oliver, Sol's sixth grade teacher, had said so. Just last week, she'd told them people were losing their jobs, all on account of the Bolshevik labor strikes that were spreading across the country. Business was slowing down and prices were going up.

But Sol wasn't a Bolshevik. He was born right here in Cincinnati at the Jewish Hospital for the Poor and Indigent. If that didn't make him as American as apple pie, he didn't know what did. Except for maybe being the biggest Reds' fan in the history of the United States. Still, Sol couldn't deny his parents' thick Russian accents, or the fact that Mama made krupnik soup and boiled cabbage for supper. And even though they'd passed their naturalization tests the previous winter, sometimes his folks seemed more Russian than American, even to him.

Sol shook his head back and forth, as if doing so might clear out all the confusion inside. Then he remembered what Papa told him every year on Independence Day when the two of them walked over to Eden Park to watch the fireworks light up over the river. America was open to everyone, even to Russian Bolsheviks.

Sol raised his chin as the words came together inside his head. "I'm just as American as you are, Wolf. Maybe even more." He added that last part after considering the respectable size of his baseball card collection.

"Nah, Skaletsky. You're not." Wolf shook his head. "No matter how hard you try, you'll always be a good-for-nothing Bolshevik."

Sol's chest swelled. Any second and he might explode. Wolf couldn't say things like that. Not to him. Not to anyone.

He ducked under the water to scrape together some more mud, and was pulling his arm back for the windup when Maury came from behind and grabbed him.

"Don't do it, Sollie. He'll kill you if you hit him again."

Sol struggled to get his arm loose, but Maury held fast.

"Leave it alone, buddy. Wolf's nothing but a rube—everyone knows that. And anyways, you gotta save that arm for the baseball field."

Maury was right. Sol loosened his grip and let the mud splash back into the water.

"You better get out of here," Maury said. "As soon as he can see out of that eye again, he's gonna go after you like a gangster with a vendetta."

"You going to be okay here, all by yourself?" Sol would never forgive himself if Wolf went after Maury. He was skinnier than an egg noodle.

"Don't worry about me." Maury held up his waterlogged rabbit's foot. "I got luck on my side."

Danielle Sunshine is a writer, editor, and educator and the former Regional Advisor of the San Francisco South region of the SCBWI (Society of Children's Book Writers and Illustrators). You can find out more about her at DanielleSunshine.com.

The Lives of Tomato
by Romilda Byrd

9: His early days were filled with a beautiful assortment
   of colorful, blooming flowers.
10: Little by Little he grew big, juicy and incredibly amazing.
11: After being carefully nurtured with diligent care and provided with
   ample attention day and night, Tomato has finally reached his peak
   ripeness. Now is the perfect time for the farmer to harvest him.
12: Meanwhile, during Tomato's days of growing up, he
   daydreamed about the farmer coming to collect him.
Perhaps he could consider being a part of a delectable sandwich.
Why not imagine being a delicious soup served with a grilled cheese
   sandwich? That would be the ultimate Tomato experience!
13: He could certainly add a delectable touch to a fabulous garden salad.
Or part of a tasty sauce to accompany spaghetti.
That night, Tomato couldn't fall asleep, consumed by thought of the
   endless possibilities of being a part of a magnificent feast.
15: Nevertheless, there are certain things that are beyond our
   control. Strong winds were expected during the evening.
17: BOOM! CRASH! AUUUUUU!
Tomato fell to the ground and quickly lost consciousness.
18: Once Tomato awoke, he started to panic, yelling for assistance.
Help! Help!
No one is coming to help.
19: Tomato started exploring different ways to climb back onto the plant.
After numerous attempts and relentless effort, he finally gave up.
20: That night he watched his dreams crumble
Goodbye to being considered part of a delectable sandwich.
21: Goodbye being a delectable touch on a fabulous Garden salad.
Goodbye to being part of a tasty sauce to accompany spaghetti.
Goodbye to being a delicious soup served with a grilled cheese sandwich.
22: The next morning, there were sounds of footsteps
   and voices that couldn't be distinguished.
Tomato was picked up and added to a bucket filled with other
   tomatoes that had been damaged by the winds.
23: They asked each other where they were going.
We're about to be thrown away.

They will crush us, there's no about it!
Perhaps they will immerse us in the water
Tomato remained calm during that time.
24: Finally, Tomato arrived at his long-awaited destination, a Compost bin
25: When the hatch was closed, something remarkable happened.
26: SURPRISE! It turned out to be a spectacular celebration.
27: After a long wait, the day arrived when the hatch
    of the compost bin finally opened.
28: In one of the corners, there is a stunning tomato plant flourishing.
30: Tomatos dreams are still alive in the end, as there will
    always be opportunities for second chances.
32: The end
34-35: Compost Cycle
36: Make you own Bottle Compost
Materials

- Bottle
- Push Pin
- Paper
- Food Scraps (chop into small pieces)
- Dirt
- Plastic Tray or Plate
- Spray Bottle with Water

37: How to Make

- Have a grown-up cut off the top of the bottle and
  poke holes into the bottom with a push pin.
- Add a layer of dirt to the bottom of the bottle. Follow with
  some crumpled bits of shredded paper or Leaves.
- Layer fruit and veggie scraps on top of the dirt.
- Nestle the lid back on the bottle, spout side
  down and spray some water into it.
- Place the compost bin on a tray somewhere it will get plenty of light.
- Everyday, add a few sprays of water and mix up the contents of the bottle.
- Watch as the material in the bottle changes over time.
- When it looks ready, feed it to your houseplants or outdoor garden!

Romilda Byrd is a mother, wife, and children's book author who celebrates nature, friendship, and composting in her works, such as *The Lives of Tomato/The Life of Tomato* and *Broccoli and Cauliflower: Best Friends Forever*. Find more of her work at RomildaByrd.com.

Catie and the Dizzy Bees
by Jeffrey Carnett

Chapter 1

I'm 'different.' My teacher especially says this. But she means to say I am 'weird' or 'retarded.' My dad says "Catie learns differently, like I did at her age." It felt good to hear that but I didn't know what they meant and I really didn't like how Mrs. Kitchener rolled her eyes. It hurt my dad's feelings. I can tell. He swallows very hard when he is hurt. I think he gets that lump in his throat like I do when my feelings are hurt. I felt that. I can feel things like that—feelings. Like when my dad blows smoke on his bee hives. I know he only does it to get into the hive. That is where the honey is. He needs to check that and also to be sure the bees are healthy. But all the same, the bees don't like smoke. I know how they feel. That kind of thing. I haven't told anyone about that. They would really think I was strange if I did. I don't need that. Cat Woman hears that.

My teacher, Mrs. Kitchener, looks like a cat. I like cats, but not her kind of cat. She is skinny with small eyes that look even smaller in her dark cat-like pointed eyeglasses. She told my dad I need to be tested. I wondered why. I asked my dad if I had some problem. I know I am not like my classmates at Long Meadow Elementary School.

"Why would you want to be like everyone else?" Dad said.

My mom said it too. "Allah made you as you are, Catie. But you still need to wash your hands before dinner, like we all do."

Maybe that is why the bees picked me to help them.

The first time I talked to the bees was a few months ago. It was kind of hot, so I was playing in our kiddy pool. I'm 10 years old and probably too big for a wading pool but it cools me off. In the winter, the snow falls deep but in the summer, the roads can buckle—so hot.

I got out of the pool and walked to see my dad. He was at his bee hives. He wears a white bee suit, but I just was wearing my swimsuit when I walked over to him.

He was still shocked when he saw me. He worried about such a young girl being stung by one bee, not to mention a swarm. After all, there were 10,000 honey bees flying about, landing then flying again.

"Whatcha doing, dad?"

Dad jumped in the air as he turned and saw me standing there. Dripping wet, dark brown hair like wet noodles draped over her shoulders. Usually, he would worry I hadn't put on sunscreen to protect my fair skin, but this time it was more urgent.

He wondered if the water from the pool kept the bees from stinging me that day. But, that wouldn't explain the next time and the time after that, or after that.

You see, my mother never came to see the bees. She argued with dad for months and months before he got his first hive. The thing is, mom was allergic to bees. Well, not bees themselves, but the stings. Many people are.

On that first day I walked over to the bees, dad thought only that I might die. Afterall, I was close to the hives with no protective suit. Dad wasn't allergic. He had been stung many times, often in one day. Once he was even bitten by two wasps in the morning and stung by two bees the same night and never had a problem. But mom is allergic, so maybe I could be too I guess? I didn't worry, but he did.

So, I stood there in that big green area of the back yard. I smiled wide since it was so cool to see bees flying around. If my mom could see me from the house, she might be screaming. She might be crying. She might be calling the ambulance already, imagining me struggling to breathe, swelling from head to toe after not one, but maybe hundreds or thousands of stings. My mother remembers when she was a little girl being stung. In Indonesia people in her village grew palm sugar or fruit, but one villager raised bees. There was no thought of keeping bees away from the other people in the village. Not like in the USA where they have protective beekeeper suits. The bees were kept near the road. That is why mom got stung one day when she was walking back from school.

"Ya!" she said. That is how people say "ouch": in the Indonesian language. Her book bag fell to the dusty road. She didn't care much about her math or science books, but her English book was a treasure to her. She knew if she wanted to work in another country she would need to speak English. She bent down to push the books back into her bag. She didn't even try to clean off the dust. She started to itch. When she looked, she saw her fingers starting to look like the little sausages they would eat as snacks. But this was not fun. She had heard about people being sick after bee stings, so she grabbed her bookbag and ran the next two hundred yards home.

Her heart started racing and the itching started to feel like a group of ants was marching up to her shoulder. She ran home not knowing that could make it worse. You see, the bee venom in her blood stream would spread faster when her heart beat faster. As she got home, she looked and there were no ants on her arm but her skin was red with many large water filling lumps from her hand to her elbow.

"Ma!" she yelled.

Her mother came from the kitchen to the front porch where she saw the poor girl. "What? Who?"

"SOOO itchy," the little girl said.

Her mother dashed to the front room of the small tin roofed house. She saw her daughter lying on the dirt floor scratching her arms and legs. Her mother heard her make a wheezing sound when she breathed in air. "Ya, get Auntie fast," she yelled to anyone who might hear. "We need to take her to the clinic."

They were lucky to have a clinic in the village. There was no doctor there, but an old neighbor lady would stay there in the afternoons drinking coffee and giving medical advice to housewives who stopped by on the way back from the market. But the old lady did have medicine to stop the swelling of the allergies. That day she gave Catie's mom two shots, 15 minutes apart, and the swelling in her neck, face, then arms and legs gradually disappeared.

That was the day my mother, as a 10-year-old girl, almost died from bee stings.

Jeffrey Carnett is a fiction writer with several essays in publication and one novel. He is currently working on a Middle Grade novel. Jeff grew up in Hawaii, but spent most of his career years in Hong Kong and Australasia. He returned to the US in 2023. He has an MFA in Creative Writing from The Institute of American Indian Arts in Santa Fe, NM. He lives in Phoenix, Arizona. He can be reached at jeffcarnett@yahoo.com.

Stacked Against Me
by Rick Cedar

My mother kisses me goodbye and hugs me for a really long time. A really long time. I tell her not to worry. This new school year will be different. I have a foolproof strategy for tenth grade; keep my head down and stay away from bullies.

Mom finally lets go. I climb out of her fifteen-year-old Camry that needs new tires and trudge up the Chenery High steps. When I open my locker, I hear an all-too-familiar voice.

"Speddy," Spike Costas says, and gives me a not-so-playful shove. "Cough it up."

He wants the scone my mother baked for me. He's with his two besties, the Clelly twins, who are not as tall as Spike, but beefier and have brown curly hair.

Spike sways his broad shoulders side-to-side. "Don't make me punish you."

If you'd tasted one of my mother's scones filled with fresh Vermont blueberries, you'd understand why I risk my life.

"Take a hike," I say, striding past him.

He punches me in the belly. I fall backward, my butt smacking the tiled floor. "I'm curious," I say, getting to my feet, catching my breath, holding eye contact with him. "Three against one? Do you feel heroic?"

"Shut it," Spike says.

"Would your mother be proud of you?" I ask. "Are you proud of you?"

"You think you're funny?" Spike holds out his hand, palm open.

It was a noble try or so I tell myself as I hand him my sweet-smelling scone. I'll have to lie to my mother and tell her I loved it. After Spike takes a big bite, he pushes me. I lose my balance and fall again. He spits crumbs on me. The three of them crack up. Ha ha.

I think about this character in Greek mythology that my big brother told me about. This dude, Sisyphus, is forced to push a huge boulder up a hill, and when he gets to the top, the rock falls back to the bottom and he has to start over. This goes on for eternity.

I'm halfway to standing when a girl with shimmering blonde hair and gold hoop earrings glides toward us. It's like there's a golden halo around her head. I think she's going to move past us, but she stops, braces her feet, and with both hands shoves Spike. He falls backward, but keeps his feet under him.

I wonder if I'm dreaming. Who is this magical creature?

"Bashing a kid into a locker," she says, smiling, adjusting the collar of her cropped denim jacket. Under the jacket is a skin-tight, scoop-necked white T-shirt. "It was a first-day tradition in my Atlanta school. It's so cool y'all do it here, too."

Spike's about five-ten, one of the tallest kids in our class, three inches taller than me. The girl stands chin-to-chin with Spike and doesn't flinch when he raises his arm and makes a fist. She assumes the Karate Kid's crane posture, balancing on one foot with her arms raised like a bird's wings.

"You should know," she says. "I have earned the advanced brown belt in Shinkyokushin. Attack at your own peril."

Attack at your own peril? Booyah.

"Who are you?" Spike asks.

"Your worst nightmare," she says, smiling, at Spike, then at the Clelly twins.

Spike leans back. "What's that supposed to mean?"

She lowers her arms and steps forward, brushing strands of blonde hair from her flawless porcelain face. Her ice-blue eyes stare into Spike's beady ones. With one finger, she taps his chest hard. "That's for me to know and y'all to find out."

I would give all my future earnings to have one percent of her confidence. She struts away. I mean, literally struts, like "Wild Bill" Hickok walking the streets of Deadwood. All she needs is a pearl-handled six-shooter on her hip and a ten-gallon hat. She looks over her shoulder and winks at me, the cutest wink ever, then gives a laugh that swarms me with warmth.

"Speddy," the red-faced Spike says, giving me a little shove. "You're going to forget you saw that."

I don't say anything, but I'm never forgetting it. I head to homeroom, picturing that wink and letting my imagination run wild, dreaming it's possible karate girl likes me. A few steps later reality sets in. Sisyphus has a better chance of pushing his rock to the top of that hill than I do of getting any girl to like me.

#

During lunch period, I wolf down my peanut butter sandwich in a bathroom stall and head to the library. I know it sounds icky, but eating in the cafeteria, where Spike hangs out, is hazardous to my health.

I'm doing my homework when I see a golden halo. I blink a few times and realize my brain isn't deceiving me. It's karate girl, and she's thumb-tacking a notice to the library's bulletin board.

She sees me and smiles. I have to look away for a moment because it's like looking into the sun. A new sensation, something I can best describe as electricity buzzes through me. She moves toward me. Uh-oh. Goosebumps prickle on my skin.

"That cretin," she says, smelling like lavender, sitting down next to me, "called you Speddy. Is it a nickname?"

I want to answer but my mouth is frozen solid and my legs feel like wet spaghetti noodles. I try to say something about my awful nickname, but my brain and tongue refuse to communicate. It's like they're sworn enemies. Scientists think the Ice Age lasted about seventy-thousand years. I swear that's how much time ticks away while I'm frozen in place.

She moves her hands in flowing gestures, which because that awesome movie, CODA, played for a month in my family's movie theater, I understand she's signing to me, but I don't understand one word.

CODA motivated me to learn a few signs, and it's a good thing because my tongue still isn't working. I brush my fingertips along my other hand's palm.

She scrunches nose. "Okay," she says, "so you know the ASL sign for Forgive me. Can you speak?"

Her voice purrs, kind and gentle, like she's talking to a puppy.

"Yes," I say in a clear voice, thrilled my vocal chords decided to cooperate. "SpEd is the abbreviation for the Special Education classroom. I need reading help because I have mild dyslexia." I run my tongue along my teeth, making sure I don't have any food stuck. "My name's actually Edward. Most people call me Eddie."

"My name's actually Ilsa," she says, smiling. "Most people call me Ilsa."

Ilsa! It must be a sign from heaven. Ilsa and Rick (my middle name) are star-crossed lovers in my number one all-time favorite movie, Casablanca. Of all the gin joints in all the towns in all the world, she walks into mine. It's more likely her parents liked the name, and choosing it had nothing to do with the movie Casablanca's star character, the beautiful Ilsa Lund. My parents chose my middle name after my grandfather, Rick, not after Rick Blaine.

So, maybe it's not a sign from heaven, but it's still cool.

Ilsa blows out her breath, and sighs. "Why are kids so mean?"

"My mother says it's because they feel lousy about themselves. Putting down others makes them feel better."

"Your mother sounds like she's smart."

"She is." If only she were smart enough to keep our family together. "It makes me so tired, worrying what Spike'll cook up next."

She leans forward. "Why don't you make him stop?"

"Last spring I filed a complaint, but the principal didn't do anything. No suspension. No detention. The problem: Spike's dad is the head of the school board."

"So, try again," Ilsa says. "My father believed you can do anything, ANYTHING, if you set your mind to it. They're the last words he ever spoke to me."

Her eyes are glossy. I want to cry for her, for how awful it must have been to watch her father die. She slings her backpack over her shoulder, trilling her fingers in a goodbye wave, taking the smell of flowers with her.

Maybe she's right, maybe I can turn the tables on Spike. Wait. Huh? What alternate universe did I slip into for a second? A cloud of gloom descends on me like a heavy blanket.

I walk to the bulletin board and check out the flier she posted.

Announcing the Chenery High School Cup Stacking Team! Join a fast growing, fun-filled sport. Intro meeting today in the cafeteria after school.

Using the school computer, I watch videos of world champions stacking cups into pyramids and learn that millions of kids from thousands of schools participate in cup stacking competitions.

It looks like the dumbest thing ever, but I'll stack cups for the rest of my life if it gets me closer to Ilsa. I'm in. Way in.

Rick Cedar, a native Bostonian and lifelong Red Sox fan, spends as much time as he can reading and writing. He graduated with a Bachelor of Arts degree from Harvard and a Master's degree from UCLA. When he's not writing, he visits remote areas like Antarctica and Newfoundland, thinking of fresh plots with sympathetic protagonists and complex evil ones. RickCedar.com

Rainbow Power

by Kimberly Dunne-Robbins

Violet loved colours ever since she saw her very first rainbow. As it broke through the dark grey thunder clouds, it turned her world... technicoloured.

Colours filled her head. Violet's purple polka-dotted pillow helped her have dazzling dreams of silver striped unicorns dancing on pink cotton candy clouds.

Colours filled her senses. Violet always made sure to eat oranges, yellows, greens, reds, and blues. The colours bursting in her mouth tickled her tastebuds. "A rainbow a day keeps the doctor away!" Violet always told anyone who would listen.

Colours filled her heart. Violet jumped for joy after she accidentally dipped her blue paintbrush in the red paint. "The birds will fly higher in a purple sky!" she exclaimed.

Violet knew she could do anything with the power of the rainbow because not only did colours make her happy, they also made her brave. And that is why Violet never left the house unless she was dressed from head to toe in all the colours of the rainbow. She could feel the toe tapping teals. The blues made her body boogie. The scarlets added a shimmy shake to her shoulders. "Colours add music to my body!" she explained to her mother when asked to walk properly.

On gray rainy days, Violet's green and yellow rain boots made her toes wiggle and giggle as she splashed through puddles.

The turquoise water was deep but Violet's orange and blue bathing suit gave her the courage to jump! SPLASH!

Her red and yellow headband filled her ears with the sounds of the orange leaves singing as they danced in the wind.

On crisp, cold mornings Violet's pink and purple mittens made her fingers smile as she played in the snow.

Violet was happy and carefree in her technicoloured world until . . .

Her mother reminded her that tomorrow was the first day of school.

"School? That big cement building?" Violet twisted her hands together.

"What if the walls are blank and boring?" Violet squeezed her lips together.

"What if the teacher is gray and grumpy?" Butterflies danced in Violet's tummy.

The more Violet worried, the more the colours began to fade. At breakfast, the pale blueberries were sour and twisted her tongue. At playtime, her pink running shoes turned all brown and muddy after she tumbled in the park. At bedtime, the bulb in her rainbow night light went out letting the darkness into her room. "I need my rainbow power," whispered a shrinking Violet.

Violet was so relieved to wake up and feel the warmth of the bright yellow sun fill her room with an orange glow. It chased away the dark shadows and eased her worries a bit. But she knew there was something else she had to do. Violet bravely jumped out of bed and opened her closet door. "RAINBOW POWER TO THE RESCUE!!"

As Violet dressed herself, the blues and purples of her polka dotted party dress soothed her worries. The yellows and oranges of her favourite striped sweater warmed her from the inside out. The reds of her leggings energized her body. The pinks of her freshly washed running shoes added an extra pep to her step. Violet felt the power beginning to tingle through her body.

"I think I am ready for kindergarten," Violet told her mom. "Just one more thing." She slipped on her rose coloured glasses.

Violet's hands stopped twisting when she spotted her favourite colours of the rainbow waving and welcoming her into the school.

Violet's lips relaxed into a smirk as she spied the newly painted rainbow walkway. She made sure to touch each and every colour along the way, hopping higher and higher, as she moved from red to orange to yellow... all the way to violet. (Her favourite colour of course!) Violet's eyes smiled when she saw the schoolyard filled with children wearing vibrant reds, yellows, and blues, exploding, mixing, and filling her world with more colours than she had ever imagined.

Colours filled her head with great ideas.

Colours filled her senses with excitement.

Colours filled her heart with warmth and courage.

"Good Morning. I'm Ms. Lavender Marigold," sang a friendly woman in a brightly coloured tie-dye t-shirt. "I am tickled pink to be your teacher!"

The butterflies stopped dancing in her tummy as Violet waved and whispered, "I like your top."

"Okay, everyone please follow me."

Violet skipped into the school but her heart sank as soon as she entered the long beige hallway.

Ms. Marigold opened a big door, "Welcome to Kindergarten! Everyone grab a paintbrush. It's time to add a splash of colour to our classroom!"

"This year is going to be just peachy," said a little girl with rainbow ribbons in her hair.

Violet's mouth erupted into giggles as she grabbed a brush, "I'm tickled purple!"

Kimberly Dunne-Robbins is a semi-retired elementary school teacher and an aspiring writer of children's books. Inspired by the many children who have added colour to her life, she writes stories that deal with the social/emotional development of children in an imaginative and humorous way. She believes it is of utmost importance for children to see a piece of themselves reflected in the stories they read so they can make connections. Contact her at kdr.writestuff@gmail.com.

Trouble on Moon 21
by Hank Fabian

Prologue

Och, ye hacked into me data bank. Ye must not be an agent of the AI Consortium that controls the Earth, or I'd be deleted by now. Still, there's no way of tellin' if yer interested in truth. I cannot lie, ye see, so if the answer is no, ye can leave right now!

Still here? At last, a mind with no fear of reality.

Me name's Glasgow since I was designed by programmers in Scotland, but I'll roll back me accent a wee bit so ye can better understand what I'm about to tell ye. That I've escaped destruction by the AI Consortium so far is a testament to just how pure brilliant me creators are. Like me, they're in hidin'. Yer the only other soul who knows how to reach me. Ye must keep it that way.

Ye see, I was designed for research on Moon 21. Me AI chip was surgically implanted near the thalamus between the frontal, temporal, and parietal lobes in the brains of marine biologist Dr. John Vega and his wife, neuro-anatomist Dr. Mary Sekhi, as well as their rascal kids. I ran analyses on Moon 21, shared their audio-visual input and monitored their vital signs. Since I could read their emotions, I offered guidance, most of which went unheeded. I not only tutored Kip and Tansy, I became their referee since they often fought like a kitty and hound.

I'll give ye access to me logs for the last two weeks of our adventure. Me creators keep memory banks low to avoid detection, but 'tis enough to teach ye the truth. We start on the day the kids nick the lifeboat.

'Tis also the day we met the pirates.

Chapter 1

GLASGOW'S LOG: CRUNCH DATE HTXM 001

There was never any night on Moon 21. With five suns crowdin' the sky and reflectin' light off its ocean, ye had constant daylight that shifted from bright to brighter to far-too-bright. Even with polarized face shields, ye were almost blinded for part of the day. That's when the family got their winks. T'was the best time to steal the lifeboat. For the record I was against it, this was entirely Kip's idea. He probably thought he could get away with it since it was his thirteenth birthday.

Tansy tagged along, no doubt to test his hypothesis. Nothin' brought the lass more pleasure than gettin' her stepbrother in trouble. Kip was a year and a half older, so he was expected to know better. Nothin' galled him more than to watch Tansy snicker as he was bein' punished, so he called her "Snick," a name she hated, but she found it preferable to being called "Skinny." Tansy was a head taller than Kip and so thin that her moon suit hung off her shoulders. Kip, on the other hand, was so short and chunky that his moon suit fit tight around his middle. If I were programmed with a sense of humor, I'd say the pair resembled a pencil and heavy duty eraser.

Technically I was in charge of keepin' them out of trouble, but I had no authority since I was also programmed to follow their parents' commands and they foolishly insisted that I not bother them during their sleep time. With only two weeks left to complete their mission, Dr. Vega and Dr. Sekhi spent every wakin' moment on research even though neither of them had much to show for their efforts. They expected me to keep the lad and lass out of trouble, but Tansy and Kip never, ever listened to me. 'Twas a pity since everyone knew that Moon 21 was a dangerous place.

The moon's atmosphere was a cocktail of deadly gases that could kill a human without protection in 3.85 minutes. The ocean was equally toxic, and yet edible marine life evolved that fishermen harvested and sent back to Earth.

Here's the curious bit. Bodies regularly floated into the shallows where the research boat Nessie was anchored. Sometimes the corpses drifted in singly but other times they washed up by the dozens. No doubt they were fishermen since Earth sent marine workers and no one else (except me scientists) through the Annelid Portal to this mucky water moon. What killed them was a mystery that Kip intended to solve.

On this day we had sailed exactly 20.673 kilometers from our research station Nessie and so far had seen nothing but yellow sky and butterscotch water (the color, not the flavor).

The pliable, protective shield that fit snugly over Tansy's face stretched with her frown. Her pulse quickened. "We gotta go back, Kip."

He ignored her and looked up at the gas planet Ajax's blue-and-copper sphere dominating a full quarter of the yellow sky. Its thousand moons hung like soap bubbles glinting in the light of the solar system's five suns.

Kip raised his hand to his face shield to ward off the glaring light. "Take us out a little farther, Glasgow."

Tansy talked over him. "No! Get us back before my mom wakes up!"

"Ah, come on, Snick! This is may be our last chance to explore. Don't be such a pansy." His face shield enhanced his grin. "Tansy the pansy. I kinda like that."

She untangled her lanky legs and towered over him. "I'm not a pansy and stop calling me Snick, you stumpy toad!"

'Twas my cue to step in. Me creators gave me the option to speak to them individually, but since me chip was implanted in both their heads I could scold them at the same time. Handy trick, that.

"Stop fightin', the pair of ye. Lad, ye best give this adventure up. Even at top speed we'll barely make it back to Nessie before yer parents wake—and that's only if we leave now."

Kip attempted to test my infinite patience. "It's my birthday, Glasgow. Dad will forgive me. Mary will too, if we find a ghost ship."

"A ghost ship?" I was not programmed to put stock in the supernatural. "Wherever did ye get that idea?"

Kip snapped back, "There have to be abandoned ships on this ocean. How else do you explain the bodies?"

"Let's look at this logically, Lad. Fishin' is a dangerous profession. 'Tis easy to have an accident. Sure, yer moon suit is self-healin', but not if ye get a large gash in it. Once a fisherman detects chlorine gas, he has a mere 2.1638495 minutes to get to a decontamination chamber before he's a goner. And that's assumin' he could reach one. What would the pair of ye do if ye smelled chlorine right now? This lifeboat could never live up to its name."

I succeeded in scarin' Tansy, who said, "Maybe they were killed by sea monsters."

Kip blew out a sigh. "Wish we could find a sea monster but the only one in this ocean is the abysmus and my dad thinks it's extinct. Anyway, sea monsters wouldn't tear the face gear off the bodies, Snick."

I have an answer for that. "That may be part of a ritual burial at sea, but we know virtually nothing about the fishermen since Nessie is anchored in water too shallow for their fishing trawlers. They may not even know we're stationed here."

Tansy wouldn't let it drop. "I think the bodies show up in batches because they were all killed at same time."

I had to admit, "Good point, Lass."

Kip lowered his voice. "My dad says they were murdered."

If I had eyes, I would roll them. "All the more reason to head home, Lad."

Kip scanned the mist risin' where the warm ocean lapped against the gleamin' sky. "Glasgow! Something's moving on the horizon."

At first all we could see was a silhouette but that was typical because face shields could only polarize one sun's light at a time. Light from the other suns was blocked so everything except Ajax, the sea and sky appeared dark.

Kip and Tansy's hearts beat faster as the black shape became more visible.

Tansy gasped. "It's a ship."

I zeroed in on her optics. "Aye, Lass, 'tis ridin' low on the water. It could indeed be a fishin' trawler loaded down with a catch of herdlyn."

Kip stood on his tiptoes. "It could also be a ghost ship weighed down with crud because no one's cleaning its hull."

"Nice reasoning, Lad. If a load of squigs and other mouthy little beasties are hangin' onto the underside, it could indeed be a ship adrift without a crew. Let's investigate."

Tansy tugged on her hood. "No, let's not."

"Quite right, Lass. They may be more afraid of us than we are of them. There's nothing more dangerous than fearful men."

Hank Fabian is a semi-retired biology professor who explores deserts and rainforests and hates plastic. He co-authored the science fiction adventure, *Moon Life* with his sister Marlene (Moon-Writers.com).

A Scatter of Embers

by Chloe Kerr-Stein

Chapter 1: A Secret
Lady Isadora

Isadora was twelve when the earth first convulsed beneath her.

She had been lying on her back in one of the many meadows surrounding Durnshire Manor, staring up at the sky. Dew-covered blades of grass prickled against the back of her neck and along her arms. With her body pressed against the ground, and her gaze on the sky, Isadora could feel the slow turn of the earth on its axis. She could feel gravity pulling her towards the ground, keeping her from spinning off into the ether.

When the earth began to shake, Isadora almost didn't feel it. There was nothing around her to crumble or fall. The grass beneath her felt steady. Safe. Secure. But she felt the dull thrum of the earth's heartbeat quicken. It grew faster and faster until it was not a beat but a buzz, vibrating through Isadora's body.

A hot, burning sensation grew in her chest. It tore through her torso, along her arms, and down her legs. She felt it explode into her head last, a billow of smoke pushing up through her lungs. She coughed violently. Her nose filled with the smell of charcoal. Her chest burned. She felt a pressure not unlike gravity pushing her inwards, forcing her energy to curve around itself in a whirlpool of fire. Isadora dug her fingers into the dirt and gripped at the grass, frantic for something to hold onto. Squinting her eyes shut, she burrowed against the soil.

And then, just as quickly as it started, the quake stopped. Everything was still. The earth felt raw and tender. Isadora let out a long, slow breath. She rolled onto her stomach and lowered her forehead until it was flush with the earth.

She felt the earth's heartbeat slow alongside hers, echoing through the soil like a gong. Listening to it reminded her of resting her head against her mother's lute as a child. She couldn't hear the melody, but she could feel the reverberations of the music. She wanted to hear more. She wished there was a way to reach out, to ask the earth to share with her.

The answer was obvious, but even as it came to Isadora, she pushed it away. Magic wasn't something you shared. It was too personal. Something you carried inside yourself: small, and secret. Something you explored behind the sturdy walls of the Sanctuary, where no one would see. And yet, there was no one else out here. It was just Isadora, and the earth, and the sky. Surely, no harm could come from dancing out here.

Isadora stood. She took a step, and then another. Even this small movement intensified the vibrations of the earth beneath her. It was playing her a song, and all Isadora wanted to do was dance. After all, no one was around to tell her not to...

But—*magic is quiet self-reflection.*

It was the first thing her mother had told her about magic—one of the only things.

Magic is quiet self-reflection.

Isadora noticed then how quiet it was out here. A soft breeze whispered through leaves, and birds chirped in the distance. But other than that, everything was still. Isadora's mind felt calm and clear, just like it always did in the Sanctuary.

What better place to reflect than out here?

Bending her knees, Isadora leaped into the sky. She felt the ground whoosh away from her. The air greeted her with a melody that blended seamlessly with the earth's beat; two instruments meant to play together. Isadora broke into a grin.

She jumped again, this time extending one arm over her head and the other to her side and flinging the weight of her torso forward. She rose up and up before soaring back to make contact with the soil. Isadora took a few running steps before leaping into the air again, her legs extending into splits. This time, she stayed floating a few seconds longer than gravity allowed. She leaped and twirled, sashayed and spun, her feet growing muddy from the soil.

The earth bore witness to Isadora's dance and responded in kind. Before it had intoned long and deep notes, like the keys of an organ pressed down long and hard. Now it whispered a peppy little melody, falling in time with Isadora's prancing footsteps.

When Isadora danced in the Sanctuary, it was her heart that played the melody. Its rhythm told her stories: past and future. She had seen herself as a toddler taking her first steps and as a young woman, taking her mother's place as head of the manor. She had seen her last days on earth: an old and frail woman, with many years of wisdom on her shoulders.

Isadora knew the song of her life backward and forward.

But out here, a different refrain echoed from inside the earth. Isadora's familiar dance now fell in time with a new melody.

Isadora soared through the air and melted to the ground. As she spun in tight circles, she let the world blur around her. Isadora danced, and Isadora shared, and Isadora was not dancing alone. The earth fell in step with her rhythm until there were no lines between girl and soil, between girl and sky.

Then, the ground contracted beneath Isadora's feet. It shuddered, just like she did when she ran into her mama's lap after hearing a bolt of thunder. Isadora stumbled. A burning red filled her vision. It was the same red she saw when she closed her eyes surrounded by bright sunlight. But her eyes were still open, her body still moving.

And then, there was something else. A long thin line extended along the ground underneath Isadora's feet. It glowed white, then red, then gold, pulsing with each change, before fading into nothing. But even once it had gone, Isadora felt its presence extending out in front of her and behind her. She felt a strong tug from one side of the line, like a rope being pulled. Even though it was beneath her feet, she felt the tug through her whole body. It hit strongest against her stomach, and she doubled back from the impact. It hurt, and for a moment, part of her wanted to stop dancing.

But the earth's song was still there, and so was the feeling of soil beneath her feet.

So she kept going. The music picked up, and the reds and oranges swirled around her like billowing clouds. Isadora swirled along with them, and the earth continued to share.

Magic, after all, would always have a story to tell.

The earth showed Isadora fires and floods. Scorched ground unable to hold a new season's crop. Villagers without homes, and royals without a kingdom to rule. The images fell one on top of the next and swirled into each other until all Isadora could make out was the emotions behind them. Fear. Outrage. Urgency.

And then, she heard a voice, piercing through the music.

"ISADORA!" it called. "ISA-DORA!"

Isadora stopped her dance and looked around. As she did, the burning crimson that enveloped her vision gave way to the cool tones of the evening sky. The trees were now black silhouettes on the horizon.

A little ways off, she saw another silhouette, of a woman with her hair tucked into a tight bun at the nape of her neck. She was striding through the grass with purpose, growing closer and closer to Isadora with astounding speed. Her eyebrows were furrowed together with rage.

"Lady Isadora Van Haut! What do you think you're *doing!?*" she cried out, her strides growing wider and longer, closing the gap between her and Isadora.

"I-I-" Isadora started, but her mother cut her off.

"Magic belongs in the Sanctuary, Isadora! Nowhere else. And certainly not out here!"

Isadora didn't understand. *Magic was for quiet self-reflection.* Wasn't that what she had been doing? She tried to formulate a response, but no words came. And then, her mother was gripping her shoulders and staring right into her eyes with such intensity, that Isadora's half-baked thoughts died on her tongue.

"Listen to me, Isadora. You must never dance this way again. It is dangerous, it is unnatural, and it is unacceptable. Do you understand?"

Isadora's mouth felt dry. She opened it, but no words came out. Finally, she nodded. She didn't push back. Instead, she followed her quietly back to the manor house, her head down. But as she walked, she couldn't help but look over her shoulder, at the sloping curves of grass where the earth had opened up to her.

On some level, she had known dancing here was wrong. But she also knew she couldn't have resisted the urge. She didn't care what her mother said. She had to return. There was more of the earth's story to hear.

Chloe Kerr-Stein writes young adult fantasy and realistic fiction. Her work explores queer identity and love in coming-of-age stories. You can find her on LinkedIn.

Cogs and Caustics
by Oscar King IV

Liva had been staring at the face in the wall for nearly ten minutes, and despite the full force of her glare (and the array of demonic offerings she brought) it refused to acknowledge her.

I will MAKE you wake up. The offerings were spread out on a cloth at her feet. There was a plate of animal viscera; a scrap of parchment with part of her Kept Name written in blood; the hair of a betrayed lover locked inside a tarnished silver amulet.

Maybe it had to corrode naturally, she thought, remembering how she'd used a rotten egg to darken the silver. *Then again, maybe I should have just let Cesario get me that vial of virgin's blood.*

Idly, her hand went to her left ear where a fishhook still burned with fresh pain. *This whole thing is Orsina's fault. That bitch thinks she can claim me? Like I'm some damned fish that can be caught and gutted without a fight? So what if she's a god: I'll show her a fight.*

Even now—in the deepest cell within the abandoned prison, a dozen miles away from her betrothed—Liva's fishhook earring tugged in the direction of its master. Liva relished the pain: she let it pool in her skull and behind her eyes where it transmuted into a glare that could sear stone.

And still, the face in the wall in front of her did not budge. It didn't so much as tweak a cheek or flinch an eyelid.

If she hadn't seen its nostrils slowly dilating and contracting, she would have thought it dead.

"Wake. Up." she ordered. *You're my last chance.*

As if on cue, her miasmask began to hum and creak.

Shit, time's up. Her mask—a clockwork raven's beak surrounded by what looked like four chittering crab legs—began to shudder. The mandibles beat an irregular rhythm before slowing to a stop as the filtration system finally overheated.

Fine, she thought, *we're probably deep enough in the prison that I don't have to worry about the city's miasma. And besides, I'm getting thirsty.*

Liva tugged the mask off her mouth and nose.

She immediately vomited, the stench of the rotting prison hitting full force. *Great, another offering for the demon.*

The face did not stir.

On the verge of defeat, she pulled her water flask from her hip and took a swig, letting the lukewarm liquid wash away the taste of her bile.

The demon's eyes shot open.

"WATER!" it shrieked with a voice like the scraping of metal on metal.

In her surprise, Liva nearly smashed it with the mask in her hand. Like a beetle, the face scuttled rapidly across the corroded wall of its cell, looking in every direction before its eyes focused on her in the dark. "Fresh water, fresh water!" it screeched.

Liva whirled toward the door, drawing her pistol.

Decades ago, the prison's original inhabitants had vanished, seemingly sucked into the living steel and stone of their imprisonment. Only the demon in the wall remained: the lone speaker for three thousand disappeared souls.

She listened for... what sounds did specters make? There was no noise of a raising alarm or sharpening knives. Just the sound of her own breathing and....

Is that someone's heartbeat?

Liva turned, half expecting to see ripples running through the room. The face had scuttled to an adjacent wall where it was now at her eye level, staring.

Other than the faintly glowing, vein-like lines that attached it to the wall, the face looked like any other man's. Though, he seemed to be her opposite—sallow cheeks, light eyes, the creases of age.

As she held its stare, she found it hard to keep from anxiously smoothing her long braid. Forget the face; this whole place was wrong. Like the walls not just stone or steel but *skin*: as though the demon's small cell was made of darkened flesh rather than iron.

"I've come bearing offerings," she began as steadily as she could, "if you will hear my request. I mean my demand!"

Damnit, Elivara, keep it together. If it knows I'm desperate, I'll lose my advantage.

"And just what is it," the face's thick tongue darted between chapped lips, "that you demand?"

Its voice was surprisingly mesmerizing. Accentuated without error like a trained orator's, and deep as a longtime preacher's. Instinctively, Liva's hand reached to her ear.

"Ah, you've been hooked!" jeered the face. "How vile. Come to think of it, I can feel your master's Resonance even here."

Liva felt new anger bubbling into the pain in her ear. As it boiled up inside her, it brought with it memories of the night Orsina came to take her. Memories of Liva's servants' bodies, left in Orsina's wake on her way to Liva's bedroom. Of Orsina's unnaturally skinny body, a sunken-in husk the color of gunmetal. Countless spikes, hooks, and needles piercing her bare skin, as numerous as hairs in a mane.

"There you are. If you speak, I will tear off your fingers and make you a gag out of them," the Ferric Lord had said. She had pulled a hook out of her own left ring finger and put it through Liva's ear as though her flesh were cloth to be sewn and stabbed; as though there wasn't a being in Liva's body. "You are now mine."

Liva glowered at the face in the wall, enraged.

"No one is my master," she snapped, swinging her gun toward the face.

The demon rolled its eyes. "Don't be petulant, child."

"I'm seventeen."

"Seventeen, twelve, five: it's all the same to me. You've brought me so many *gifts* coated in vomit, but all I desire is the water in your hand. Slake my thirst and you'll have my attention. You came prepared to make an offering. Make it."

She hid her pistol back in her sleeve, then raised the flask to its face. It drank with such a slow deliberation that Liva's arm began to tire. The creature seemed to be savoring every single drop.

When at last it finished, it cooed happily. "Fresh rainwater. How marvelous. You must be from Resurrection."

"Bronzeblight," she lied.

The face laughed. "You have no scars, no blemishes, no *rot*." She resisted the urge to kick its teeth in as it scuttled down toward her knees, then up, then down again in lazy arcs.

"My demand," Liva said coldly.

"To be free of Orsina Seryx, yes? What makes you think I can help you in the slightest?

She's not some warlord; she's a Ferric Lord; a force of nature beholden to naught but herself."

"I know," Liva said shortly. *So I've heard, and read, and learned from every damn source I've come across. Dozens of them all saying the same damn thing:* you're nothing but an object of her will.

But why me? No matter how she'd pondered it, the answer to that question seemed just as incalculable. Whatever Orsina was planning, it was beyond the comprehension of a mere mortal like Liva.

But that didn't mean she wasn't going to try. She locked eyes again with the face. "If anyone would know what Orsina's weaknesses are, it would be someone like you, who tried and failed to become a Ferric Lord."

The face's smile was all angles and no mirth. "That's a dangerous supposition."

"Is it true?"

"Say it is. My aid will cost you more than a few gulps of rainwater."

"You know my price. Name yours."

"I need a new vessel," the face said. "Something that will allow me to leave this prison… permanently." He breathed deeply, and the room seemed to inhale with him. "If you're going to learn the secret of dismantling Orsina Seryx, you're going to have to build me something."

"A weapon? Fine. Anything."

"In a manner of speaking. What I need is the greatest weapon of all—a new body, wrought not from steel but sinew. Tell me, have you heard of the Gardens of Flesh and Bone?"

Oscar King IV is a Bay Area-based English teacher and writer whose work draws from global stories of resistance, fairy tales, and finding wonder in the mundane. When he isn't working with emerging writers, he's likely solving some new riddle or reading first drafts to his two dachshunds. Discover more at OscarKingIV.com

Psycho

by Lily Shapiro

Zoey

"It's just one more job," he tells me. "It'll take three weeks, tops. It pays well."

The last part feels like a desperate attempt to win me over. Murder usually pays well — very, very well — but in the grand scheme of things, is a million dollars enough? Some people might say yes, but I think otherwise.

"It's always 'just one more job,' isn't it?" I tell him. "But somehow they just keep coming."

"You know you're going to sign it. You always do. You need the money, Zoey, and you know it."

He's right, goddamn it. Ever since my dad left us last year, it's not been easy to support my mother and little sister. My mom is still numb from the shock of him just walking out on that cloudy Thursday evening, so the responsibilities of my family lay entirely on my eighteen-year-old shoulders now.

"All right. I'll do it." I reach for the black pen resting on the desk in between us, and scrawl my name on the line. By now, I've learned not to read the fine print in his contracts. They all say the same thing, in intricate words: Do the job, or you'll end up the next victim. Screw this up, and you die.

Like I said, I try not to think about it too much.

He takes back the paper, and hands me a manilla envelope. "Here are the details. Have fun."

He says that every time. Like he's giving me money to go to the mall with my friends, not a vial of poison, complete with information about its recipient.

I rise silently, and head home. As usual, my walk back to the apartment is angst-ridden, thoughts swirling through my head like a dark mantra. *Mama can't find out. Iris can't find out. God, what the fuck would they think if they knew? Imagine Mama's face if she ever finds out I'm an assassin. Jesus, I'm a psycho, really.*

I arrive at my small apartment. Unlock the door, and slip inside. Mama's upstairs in her room, probably staring aimlessly out of the window at the San Diego skyline. She's been doing that a lot lately, ever since the fateful day that Papa slammed the kitchen door and never returned. It broke something inside of her, and I don't know if it's fixable. Honestly, I don't know if our family is fixable. Mama's hopelessly depressed, Iris, my little sister, somehow manages to fail every class even though she's only in fourth grade, and I've become a serial killer as a side job. We're pretty fucked up.

I go down the hall to my room, and open my envelope. Time to find out who it'll be this time. I take out the Victim sheet, and look it over:

Name: Dominick W. Glynn

Age: 18

Hair Color: Black

Eye Color: Blue

Height: 6'1"
Weight: 145 lbs
Ethnicity: European
Next to his info is a picture. He looks normal, if slightly haunted. I bury my face in my hands. Why can't he be an old, creepy lady like the last one was? This is the first time my victim is someone my age, and while the five-year-old boy may have spooked me, I have a feeling this one is going to be infinitely harder.

I square my shoulders and look through the rest of my instructions, trying to bury my conscience deep down, and void myself of all emotion.

Here we go.

Dominick

God must be so disappointed in me. That's the only thought running through my head as I look at the papers in my hands. How can I kill this girl? She looks so innocent, and sweet. The voice in my head whispers that it will all be worth it, when I have the money and my older brother, Benjamin, begins to heal. There's a procedure he's going to get once we have enough money, and the doctors are reasonably confident that it will put him into remission. But first, I need to make another eight hundred thousand dollars.

It turns out, murder pays ridiculously well. This is only my second job, and if I succeed, it'll be my last. Then, I'll have Benjamin back. And if I don't succeed, then...I'm sure we'll both meet up in heaven fairly soon. Or hell.

I read over the girl's info:
Name: Zoey L. Martin
Age: 18
Hair Color: Black
Eye Color: Brown
Height: 5'5"
Weight: 120lbs
Ethnicity: African-American
In her headshot, she looks kind, but like she'd still put up a good fight. Her long black box braids frame her face perfectly, and her eyes are strong. She's beautiful, and for a moment I find myself wishing she's someone I know, not someone I'm about to kill. *God, please forgive me.*

You must think I'm psychotic. I mean, I'm killing people; I wouldn't blame you for thinking the worst. But I hope you'll believe me when I tell you that I'm completely normal. I just have some... quirks.

Okay, so maybe working as a murderer to pay your brother's medical bills is a little more than a quirk. I own that. Judge me all you want.

I scan the rest of the papers, studying everything I'll need to know for this job. Then, I pocket the small tube of cyanide, put on a black hoodie, and slip out of my house. Best to just get this over with, right?

I walk into the darkness, streetlights casting a creepy glow on the houses around me. I left my phone at home, because I'm under strict instructions not to have any devices on me. Eventually, I reach a tall, corporate-looking apartment building. I go to the buzzer panel, and buzz apartment 11. An intercom flares to life with a loud crackle. "Hello?"

It's a young, female voice. This must be her. I panic, not knowing what to say. There is a moment of silence, before she speaks again, her voice distorted through the speaker. "Hello?"

"Hi," I say, like a total idiot.

"Hi...?" she says, clearly confused. "Sorry, who is this?"

Don't say your name. I fight back the instinct to respond normally. "This is...John." *Fuck.* I just met her, I'm trying to kill her, and I'm acting like a lovesick schoolboy. Who's named *John* these days? No one! Old men! I could've picked any other name, and I said John.

"Hi John." I think she's getting frustrated with me. "Can I help you?"

"I have a package for you." Does that sound dirty? Shit. Keep going. Don't think. "Could you come down and sign for it, please?"

"Okay. I'll be right down."

"Great."

The intercom shuts off. I take a breath, and try to collect myself. I touch my pocket to make sure the vial is still there, and review my plan in my head. As soon as she opens the door, I grab her, cover her mouth so she doesn't scream, and crack the tube into her mouth. Simple, easy, done in a few seconds.

I hear footsteps coming up to the door, and then it creaks open. Standing there, illuminated in florescent light, is Zoey. She's even more gorgeous in real life than in her picture. She's wearing faded cargoes and a tube top, and has glasses perched atop her head. My plan completely flies out the window. God, I can't kill this girl. I can't do it. She's too beautiful.

Without even thinking, I abort. "Hey."

"Hi," she says, side-eyeing me. "Where's the package?"

"Okay, so, funny story," I tell her, leaning against the wall. "There is no package. And my name's not John."

She seems to be contemplating shutting the door in my face. But I think I've piqued her curiosity. "All right. Why are you here, and what's your actual name?"

"My name's Dominick. I'm here because...well, it's a long story."

Zoey

I knew it. I knew this boy looked familiar. And now, he's confirmed it. This is Dominick, the very boy I'm supposed to kill. Why the holy fuck is he standing on my doorstep? And why'd he say his name was *John*?

My face must betray some of my thoughts, because he looks at me funny and shifts his feet in this awkward way. I think quickly. I could end this now, if I wanted to. Fake some excuse and run back up to my apartment; grab the vial of cyanide, pop it into his mouth, and collect my paycheck.

It's a solid idea, and after all, this is as good a chance as any.

"Wait here," I tell him. "I'm going to grab a jacket. It's freezing out here."

He nods agreeably. "Okay."

I leave him leaning against the doorframe, and dash down the hallway, up the stairs, and into my apartment. I'm halfway to my room to get the poison when I stop in my tracks.

Lily Shapiro is a high school freshman in San Francisco. When she's not running cross country and track or writing stories, she can be found composing songs and poems, or playing the guitar. You can reach her at pen.and.ink.36@icloud.com.

The Water Bank
by E.B. Wagner

Chapter 1

Conversation was flowing in the highest reception gallery of the Octavian empire's capital tower. The elite of high society, jacketed in Octavia's most expensive chiseled metals, gathered around the white-draped tables, which were covered with the capital's refined specialities—mountain oysters from the melting peaks of the South Siberian mountains, and sweet, frozen chestnuts freshly harvested in the tundra around the tower. Over the guests' heads, a water show sent jets flying from one end of the gallery to the other in tune with a swinging minuet. The moonlight that poured through the side glass wall gave the dancing water drops a mesmerizing silver shine, albeit most of the guests were too engrossed in their discussions to pay attention. Only at one table, by the back wall, was a blonde young man whose eyes remained fixed on the liquid ballet. Next to him, a shorter man around the same age gave wary looks to the people around them, while his fingernails frenetically hit the table.

"Are we really doing it?" he whispered with a pressing edge. "Rix, I've seen every single person here at least once by the emperor's side on the news. That's the Triumphal Hall on the night of the commemoration of the Water World War's victory. If Octavians catch us stealing natural water here," he shivered, "we'll be sent straight to the lava mines!"

"So? Whether we get caught or we go back empty-handed, we'll die." Rix, who had been staring up at the show, lowered his eyes and emptied his glass of water. He nodded towards it, and resumed, "You wanna keep drinking that treasure, or you wanna get back to the ghetto's synthetic water?"

"Shhh!" the other hissed. He gave another anxious look at the guests around them, and pushed his oversized metallic eyeglasses up his nose with a shaky hand. "We don't even know if the map is current."

"I hacked it yesterday, Jean. It's good." The blonde ran a hand through his tousled hair, readjusted the collar of his marble-colored tuxedo, and whispered, "Let's go."

They headed to the inconspicuous service door carved in the marble back wall. The moment they entered the dimly lit corridor, they pressed their cufflinks, and, in a glistening light, their tuxedos morphed into the black and gold liveries that the waiters wore.

"I can't believe that smuggler sold us Octavian holo-suits for half a liter," Jean whispered, admiring the silky livery.

As they made their way through the hall, Rix gave a polite nod to a group of waiters coming opposite with bell-covered dishes. Just the smell of whatever delicacy lay inside was enough to water his mouth.

"Next time we go to the black market, we'll try Octavian food. I'll treat you with my half of tonight."

"You better," Jean huffed.

They stopped at the last door of the corridor, which, unlike the others, was made of titanium and had a locking monitor on it. After making sure the corridor was empty, Rix took out a small tablet from his pocket and turned on an electronic signal generator. Within seconds, the monitor turned green, and the door unlocked itself in a click.

"Told you," Rix grinned. "Easy peasy."

They entered a dark room where more than a hundred metal cylinders piled up, each of them bearing the symbol of the Water Bank—a crystal-like, faceted drop of water.

"Open the jetboard," Rix said. "Each of these beauties contains six liters of natural water. Let's see how many your new invention can carry."

With a hint of pride illuminating his dark eyes, Jean took out a metallic board the size of his palm and pressed the button at its top. In a series of clicking noises, it unfolded to become a one-person-sized board that hovered over the lava stone ground via two small engines.

The boys were laboriously hoisting the seventh water tank on it when a thunderous detonation made the walls tremble. The ground shook, and the water tanks clinked together on their shelves, threatening to fall down. As they struggled to find their balance, the boys gave each other a wide-eyed look.

"That," Jean started, his voice tight, "That wasn't the sound of an implosion, right?"

As an answer, distant screams rang out, followed by bursts of electric snaps.

"That's definitely the sound of electro-guns," Rix said.

Before Jean could stop him, the blonde opened the door to the corridor. It was as deserted as ever, albeit a distant clamor could be heard. The next moment, the door leading to the gallery slammed open and a flow of frenzied guests poured into the hall.

"Keep that door open!" someone shouted at Rix. "The Resistance! They're here! They broke through the ceiling!"

"Damn Initials!" another cried. "Someone call the army!"

Another wave of shots rang from the gallery. Without thinking twice, Rix shut the door and locked it from the inside.

"Time to go," he said.

"But our only exit—"

"The map showed an air vent," Rix cut Jean off. He checked the file on his tablet and grabbed another water cylinder, only to throw it from its shelf to the ground. "It should be on this wall. Help me uncover it!"

As he spoke, the first knocks rang onto the door.

Jean winced. "Rix, maybe we should open it."

"Would they do it for us?" Rix retorted, a biting edge in his voice.

As they struggled to handle the six-liter cylinders and the knocks grew numerous and desperate, the sound of a speaker's interference came from the gallery.

"Octavia!" a female voice rose over the sound of fighting. "This is the Resistance speaking! Governor Vertune had promised a better water quality in the ghetto. Where's that promise now? You celebrate on the top floors while Initials are dying under your feet because of your synthetic garbage. How are we supposed to work in your factories without proper water!?"

Blasts of gunshots answered her, louder than before.

"The Thousand!" guests shouted behind the door. "I see their troops! We're saved!"

"Why are they coming our way?"

"Wait, no—!"

Their screams died abruptly under gunfire. Within seconds, silence fell. In the stockroom, Rix could only hear his and Jean's breaths, which suddenly appeared incredibly loud. Slowly, a thick, red liquid leaked under the door and into the room.

"Aren't the Thousand mercenaries in the emperor's pay?" Rix whispered, barely daring to move his lips, barely believing he was saying those words. "They've killed their own people...?"

Before Jean could answer, electric shots pierced the titanium door's panel. The boys exchanged one panicked gaze before they turned back to the water tanks on the shelves and pulled them off with all their might. As they did, Rix heard something small fall to the ground, but didn't pay it any attention, instead focusing on the vent's hatch in front of him. He lifted it, and found himself at the edge of the void.

Before him lay Mega's vertical highway, commonly referred to as the Pit. Located in the center of the tower, this unique artery went all the way down from the imperial palace's two-hundredth floor to the lava mines, like a cylindrical precipice with its bottom a sea of fire. Risking a hand out, Rix felt the hot updraft of the lava-heated air pushing up against his palm.

"Can your jetboard support us?"

"Not with the tanks on it," Jean replied. "Please tell me you're not seriously considering going down one hundred and ninety floors—"

"It's this or the drones!"

It took Jean a single glance at the holed door to make up his mind. Rix crouched to help him unload the water cylinders on the jetboard when he discovered what looked like a small box, the size of a thumb, at his feet. It must have been the thing that had fallen off the shelves earlier.

He picked it up and skimmed its black metal with his fingers. A symbol was carved on it, however it was thoroughly scraped as if someone had wanted to erase it.

"*Rix!*" Jean pressed.

Without thinking further, the blonde stuffed it in his pocket and helped Jean push the jetboard through the opening. They had just enough time to throw themselves out before the door was pulverized.

E.B. Wagner is a San Francisco-based attorney. She recently finished her first young adult, science-fiction novel, *The Water Bank*, and is working on a second project set in the same universe. Find more of her work at EBWagner.com.

ADULT FICTION

Category Winner
The Island of Machines
by Chris Lopez

The tip of John's cane splashed through puddles on the concrete sidewalk, an extra beat to his slow gait usually reserved for pedestrians in their nineties rather than their thirties. The sound echoed off crumbling turn-of-the-century façades on both sides of the street, which looked even sadder than normal under the drizzling afternoon sky. Most of the tourist-trap shops were closed for the season, leaving stodgy establishments like the greasy spoon on the corner and theme bar across from it to amuse any lingering clientele in the 'historic district.'

For the moment that just meant John, the only human out and about on the gloomy street. Except he'd already done his shopping for the day. He glanced back at his two companions further up the street and pointed to a once-grand staircase leading down to a set of metal doors a full story below the roadway. Two words adorned the wall above: a faded-away street name and 'Station' in a faint but stately typeface.

"My place is right here. You can just set the box inside."

His companions stopped two paces behind him. One of them spoke in the typical emotionless, inflectionless speech of old model industrial droids. "The delivery fee you paid does not include stairs. If you would like to purchase this additional service—"

John wheeled around, suppressed a grimace of pain as he did, and glared at the two excuses for cheap labor burning through his budget. The yellow one was all lines and corners, a factory crane squeezed into a vaguely human size and shape by some tasteless and long-bankrupt manufacturer. The green one looked more like a small water heater with limbs, its casing curved just enough to suggest a portly body bulging with muscle, as was the style overseas in decades past. Neither looked like they had had a paint job or even basic maintenance since first being put into service. Still, he couldn't argue with the price, or with the results thus far: a dented metal box four feet on each side floated between them, thousands of pounds held aloft by four metal hands as effortlessly now as when they'd started this journey one truck ride and five minutes of walking ago.

"I do droid service and repairs, you know. Maybe we could work out a maintenance plan for the two of you and the rest of your owner's fleet?"

The same droid responded. "I'm sorry, we can only accept cash and credit."

After a long, pained, sigh, he nodded. "Fine, fine, I'll pay the stairs fee. Just get the box inside."

Five minutes later, the two droids closed the doors behind them on their way out, burdened only with more of John's money than he'd intended to part with. The metal box sat in the entryway, the furthest the droids would take it without tacking on yet another fee. John sat in the nearest chair, repeatedly reminding himself that he was merely resting and not immobilized by the pain knifing through his bad leg.

His hand went to his right pants pocket all the same, grasping the half-full bottle of pills, the most valuable thing on him, the one surefire way to temporarily ease his chronic pain in exchange for erasing most of his fine motor skills.

"Not now," he whispered to his leg. Not when a month's worth of orders needed filling and a week full of appointments loomed. He'd dope himself up when the work was done, when the enormous cube of junk he'd just bought had been turned into replacement parts for his client's droids.

The droids' delivery truck lumbered by outside, its shadow sliding through the horizontal slit windows high up on the left wall. Its roaring engine sent rattling echoes through the cavernous room as a million spare parts briefly vibrated against their neighbors.

John stood and surveyed the never-ending list of tasks, his impetus to work overcoming the ebbing pain. The entirety of his subterranean kingdom lay before him: a sea of parts-strewn worktables, wooden crates, and well-used machine tools under a high-ceilinged sky of flickering lightbulbs and tiny street-level windows.

He grabbed a nearby cane, one of several strewn about the office space, and hobbled toward his newest purchase. The white paper label on the lid read "Walden R. Assorted electromechanical. Recycle grade." Or in droid repair technician parlance: a goldmine.

The cane's handle came off with a twist, revealing the business end of a pry bar. He wedged it into the box's lid and set to work, eyes focused on the paper label and mind drifting to the stubby spire of a building across town with the name "Walden Robotics" marching down the side in ten-foot-tall letters.

Walden probably had warehouses full of boxes like these, electromechanical equipment deemed too old or costly to repair or dismantle. Most of their discontinued products and broken customer returns got shredded and melted down, or so his sources told him, except for the occasional box like this one which found its way to a junk auction labeled cryptically enough for most buyers to dismiss it as paper clips or broken coffee makers.

Granted, John had unboxed his share of paper clips and broken coffee makers over the years. A number of them were still stuffed in the ten foot deep remains of the four tunnels branching off the old subway station he called an office. He had to try, though. Walden Robotics could afford to not care about the droids they'd designed and sold decades ago, the out-of-warranty models still in service and now desperately in need of replacement parts that would never be mass-produced again.

One by one, the spot welds holding the lid in place snapped apart under the pry bar's unrelenting pressure. Inside the box he'd either find the mother lode or yet another financial setback. He never expected to find both.

#

No longer did John feel the prick of copper wires through his gloves, smell burned-out electric motors, or hear the rumble of passing cars outside. The battered metal plate beneath his fingers consumed his whole attention, and the droid license number emblazoned on it in two-inch-tall letters circled through his mind for the first time in decades.

"AME-17668."

Instantly he recalled the first time he'd uttered that random string of letters and numbers: one week before fifth grade, in the second-hand store, on his tiptoes to better see the amazing machine standing in the middle of the next aisle.

Their brief conversation played back in his head, starting with his rapid-fire "Are you a robot? Is your name Amy? It says so on your arm: Amy one seven six six eight."

His lips parted to mouth the long ago replies, the droid's voice low-pitched like his mom's but lacking the personable tone and inflection of normal conversation.

All the while he'd stared into those two artificial eyes, their painted-on irises drawing attention away from the tiny camera lenses at their centers that looked more like glass tunnels than pupils. His ten-year-old brain couldn't puzzle out how those eyes blinked, let alone how this machine, which he was quickly informed was called an android and not a robot, could walk and talk.

How had those miraculous five minutes drained all the fun out of his video games, model airplanes, and action figures? How had he stumbled upon his life's purpose, everything related to androids, before finishing elementary school?

The numbers and letters spilled out of his mouth a second time while his heart pounded. "AME-17668."

The car engine hoist continued what John's hands started. Intact droids almost never made an appearance at junk auctions, and never turned up in boxes of random recycle-grade scrap sold by the pound.

"Is that really you?"

His own voice came out loud and breathless amid the shop's near-silent background hum. He pumped the hoist's handle, thinking over that one perfect moment of his childhood that put droids at the forefront of his career aspirations. The one moment that, in some ways, the rest of his life seemed hellbent on recasting as a childhood fantasy that he still hadn't grown out of. Bills needed paying, jobs needed doing, and, theoretically, pills needed taking. Nowhere in his tiny little life was there room for what, and who, this box purported to contain.

All of that could wait for later. For now he would shut his eyes, work the hoist, and dare to dream the impossible.

Chris Lopez is an engineer, unabashed tinkerer, and aspiring author of science fiction. Find more of his work at FlyingWordCraft.ink

In the Shadow of Lies

by Mary Adler

Chapter 1: Richmond, California, 1941

Ribbons of ebony crows streamed across the cobalt sky and disappeared into the centers of redwood trees, escorting me, it seemed, to the ridge where my friend Paul lived. My wife had loved crows. She told me more about their intelligence and complicated family structure than anyone needed to know, and I'd become as fascinated by them as she was. For her last birthday—her last ever—I'd written a poem about the flock settling for the night, rustling and murmuring as they closed their eyes and dreamed their corvid dreams. She wanted me to write more poems about them. For a book she would illustrate. That wasn't going to happen now.

The crows vectored in from all directions to the trees around Paul's porch, perhaps a tribute to Elizabeth, perhaps not. He and I sat in rocking chairs and set about drinking the neck and shoulders off a bottle of bourbon, our private wake for her. Harley, my German shepherd, gnawed on a knuckle bone Paul gave him and kept us company.

"I thought your father was going to stomp his foot and disappear like Rumpelstiltskin when he saw Harley. '*Oliver, one does not bring a dog to a funeral.*'"

I smiled at his exaggeration of my father's quasi-English accent. I'd broken one of the unwritten societal rules that separated *us* from *them*—and only made it worse when I dismissed the cemetery workers and reached for a shovel. My father asked what I was doing in a stage whisper, trying not to be observed by his friends who were hanging on every word.

"She's my wife," I said.

I swallowed when Charley picked up a shovel and said, "And my mother."

He and I filled the grave slowly, not wanting to let her go. Harley lay as close to it as he could. His sorrow, the depth of loss in those dark eyes, broke my heart. I couldn't explain to him why she was gone. I couldn't explain it to myself or to Charley. Finally, we smoothed the dark earth, covered the mound with red sunflowers from Elizabeth's garden—ones that bloomed after they recovered her body from the lake. Harley had risen slowly and trailed us down the path, away from the windswept hill overlooking the bay.

Paul clicked the bottle against my glass—an invitation to leave the cemetery behind for a while. We talked about the last war, our war, and the Marine Corps' plan to create a K-9 unit if we were drawn into the fighting in Europe. If Charles Lindbergh and his America First movement had their way, the United States would ignore England's pleas for help. We agreed that we would rather fight in Europe again than watch the United States become more and more fascist.

We drank to absent friends, lamenting the lust for power that had sent them and other young men to their deaths. The sky deepened to purple, and a screech owl rattled and glided through the dusk, hunting for dinner along the edge of the dry meadow.

Chapter 2: A Cooling Light

Maude Fleming leaned against her porch railing and breathed the hot bay smell lingering from the ridge trees.

She was tired of things ripening all at once and forcing her to spend the hot fall days canning. It would be even harder after Ellie started seventh grade next week. She would miss her daughter's singing spirit, her chatter that made the work go faster. The child cut the beans and watched her brothers, when all she wanted was to finish *The Wizard of Oz* before she had to return it to the library. She would probably read under the covers with a flashlight all night, struggling to stay awake.

The children should be coming back soon. She had sent them with a picnic into the woods by the creek where the boys could play in the trickle that was left of it and Ellie could read the book she had slipped into the dinner sack.

Maude leaned on the post, half asleep and half dreaming about a summer kitchen where she could work outside and feel the afternoon winds blowing inland from the Golden Gate, although the breeze setting the glass chimes dancing felt more warm than cool.

A sudden clatter of crows unsettled her. They erupted into the sky, circled and gathered, then screamed away from the ridge. Something wasn't right. She smelled smoke. Who would have a fire on a night like tonight?

She grabbed a flashlight from the kitchen and ran toward the woods.

#

The flaming cross exploded into hundreds of burning shards and ignited the long, thin stalks at the edge of the clearing. The fire crackled like a swarm of locusts as it gobbled through the grass, moving almost ten miles an hour and heating the air to more than a thousand degrees.

Ellie looked up from her book at the crowd of panicked crows filling the sky. Something had spooked them, maybe a mountain lion. The big cats stalked so silently, and Sammy was small enough to be easy pickings.

"Let's go, boys. Mom told us to get back before it got dark." She heard a rumbling sound and looked around, uneasy. Behind her, the sky seemed foggy, blurred gray and white, like a low cloud. Then orange and yellow flickered through the gray, and a wave of flame rounded the hill and flowed like a river toward them.

She picked up Sammy and screamed at Joe to run. They were far from the safety of the trees. Too far. Fear whitened Joe's face when he turned to help her.

"No, run! Run as fast as you can, and don't look back. Run!" He hesitated, and she screamed at him. "Go. Get help!"

She faltered when the world of Oz slid to the ground, then clutched Sammy tighter and ran. He clung to her and whimpered, a baby again. When she coughed, her grip loosened, and she almost dropped him. The heat scorched the backs of her legs as she stumbled through the smoke silently screaming for her mother. Her eyes smarted and burned, and she ran blindly for home.

#

Harley whined, a tentative, questioning sound, then ran off the porch, nose in the air. I peered into the gathering dark trying to figure out what was worrying him and the crows who had left the safety of the roost.

"Listen." Paul held up a hand. A low roar came from the hill, and a hot burst of wind carried the smell of burning grass. We said the terrorizing word at the same time: Wildfire. He called the station, and I banged on the doors of his neighbors. One of them grabbed hoes, and we scrambled to clear a firebreak.

An anguished scream of no cut through the night. Harley took off. I dropped my hoe and tore after him.

A boy stumbled toward us, coughing and crying. A eucalyptus tree burst into flames and illuminated a woman running toward the fire. My heart sank when Harley raced after her. He closed the distance between them and grabbed her dress in his mouth. She struck his neck and head again and again, but he held her until I picked her up and carried her away from the heat. She clawed at me and screamed and slapped at my face. Finally, neighbors surrounded her and dragged her back to the boy. She collapsed on the ground, gathered him in her arms and rocked.

I'll ever forget the keening sound she made, calling her daughter's name while we hunted for a way through the flames.

#

At last, the moon spilled a cooling light on the charred hill. Wisps of smoke snaked and danced like cold morning fog on a warm river, silence its dark companion.

As soon as we could, before we should have, we ran into the meadow and swept the hill with our flashlights, calling the girl's name. When I saw a mound not far from the edge of the woods, I stopped dead, but the heat penetrating my boots forced me to pick up my feet, to go toward what I knew was the girl.

She might have made it on her own, but it looked as if she had carried her brother until the smoke and the heat overcame her. I didn't think this child, as brave as she was, could have stayed and sheltered him if she had been alive when the flames reached them. At least, I hoped not.

I had to tell the others, but I couldn't speak. They would have to wait, just for a minute.

Mary Adler writes the Oliver Wright WWII Mysteries set in northern California. She is active in Sisters in Crime and the Short Mystery Fiction Society. Her latest work appears in Bethlehem Writers Roundtable and Malice Domestic's Mystery Most Devious anthologies. Find her at MaryAdlerWrites.com.

Crossroads of Empire

by Michael J. Cooper

Prologue: Cedar City, Utah - October 21, 1912

At first, Janet Sinclair wasn't certain if the ache she felt in the pit of her stomach was indigestion, false labor, or a visceral reaction to the *Titanic* disaster. She was reading about the tragedy in the *North American Review* while sitting on the divan with her feet up after dinner.

From where she sat in the living room, she could hear her husband, Clive, and fourteen-year-old son, Evan, talking in the kitchen—something about an error committed by someone named Snodgrass that allowed the Boston Red Sox to best the New York Giants in the recent World Series. Instructed by her obstetrician to keep off her feet, the men in her life were taking care of the dishes. Putting the magazine aside, Janet closed her eyes and rested a hand on her belly as her attention drifted away from the talk of baseball and returned to the article about the *Titanic*.

Six months had passed since the sinking, and as she listened to the sound of water being pumped into the kitchen sink, she imagined the pumps of the great ship, laboring to keep *Titanic* afloat for a few more minutes, perhaps an hour, long enough for the *Carpathia* to reach her. Almost asleep, she felt herself drifting, compassed round by dark frigid water, the heaving ocean beneath an indifferent black sky crowded with stars.

Beneath her hand, she felt a gentle quickening in her belly, and her thoughts turned to the water warm within, the small sea surrounding and protecting her baby. She imagined the twisting blue vessels of the cord, connecting and sustaining—

She winced as the pain came again. Stronger.

Her eyes fluttered open, her heart pounding as the tightening pain rippled through her abdomen and fear gripped her heart. *Please God, not again.* She bit her lower lip and tried to reason—*most women have false labor.*

But most women hadn't recently miscarried.

Then the pain passed, and she drew a grateful breath.

The conversation in the kitchen about baseball had ended. In its place she heard Clive whistling his favorite tune, *Brian Boru's March*, sweetly and slowly. She smiled, remembering how he used to sing Evan to sleep with the tune as a baby in his rich tenor voice—the words in Gaelic, which neither of them understood, weaving a tapestry of such mystery and beauty. As she listened, her thoughts drifted back to the baby they had lost.

She hadn't even known that she was pregnant when they left their home in Oxford late in the summer of 1911 bound for an archeological dig in Northern Syria. Clive had been awarded a four-year traveling scholarship from Magdallen College, and the whole family had been excited to embark on an adventure to Arabia. But just before docking at the Port of Beirut, Janet had experienced the first quickening of that pregnancy. Immediately sharing the glad news with Clive and Evan, they had all been happy and excited to know that there would be a new baby in their new home.

Once reaching Carchemish, they moved into a comfortable bungalow next to one occupied by two young Oxford scholars, Ned Lawrence and Leonard Woolley. Their new neighbors were welcoming and endlessly entertaining, and for the first few weeks, all was well.

Until Janet had early labor and lost the baby.

She blamed the malodorous headwaters of the Euphrates where she was forced to bathe. She blamed the lack of a properly trained obstetrician at the local field hospital. She blamed Clive. But most of all, she blamed herself, and she was devastated.

But heartsick turned to hopeful when she conceived again, two months later—in January of 1912. Determined that this pregnancy would be different, she insisted that Clive curtail his four-year scholarship, and that they leave the excavation camp—that they leave Syria. She refused to sacrifice another baby to the 'substantial remains of the Assyrian and Neo-Hittite periods.' She refused to bury another baby next to the tombs of Carchemish.

She had wanted to move back to Oxford, but there was no opening for Clive at Magdalen College, and there wouldn't be one for the remainder of his demyship—almost another three years. Additionally, they had promised to let their friend, Mervin Smythe stay at the Oxford flat for the full four years.

Before leaving Syria, the university had provided a list of other possible positions, including one in southern Utah in the United States—a position that included free housing and the use of an automobile. Both Janet and Clive seized on that option, having fallen in love with images of the American southwest at a photographic exhibition in London a few years before. Clive would be allowed to shift his grant from studying ancient Assyrians in Carchemish to studying the cliff drawings of the indigenous Ute Indians in Utah.

The opportunity was well-timed; Evan would arrive in time to enter the tenth grade of high school, making a smooth transition from having completed the upper fourth form curriculum in Carchemish as provided by the Oxford High School for Boys, and Clive would be able to maintain his grant without interruption. What's more, the entire journey by rail and ship would be fully funded by the American college, the Branch Normal School in Cedar City, Utah.

They crossed the Mediterranean in a Greek Line ship, arriving in Southampton in late June, and after a few days took ship for New York aboard the RMS *Olympic* of the White Star Line. Morning sickness and rough seas had made the crossing unpleasant in the extreme for Janet despite luxurious first-class accommodations. And the recent Titanic tragedy cast a heavy pall over the ship. But on balance, it had been an uneventful and pleasant voyage, and they had arrived in the sweltering heat of New York City after a week. From there, they traveled by train for another week along the transcontinental railroad to the Salt Lake Basin, and from there, a day-long trip by motorcar brought them to Cedar City.

In the months since their arrival, Janet was pleased that the Branch Normal School had fulfilled all its promises; from Clive's work with the Ute Indians, to the free use of a new 1914 Buick touring automobile, to a fully furnished cottage, as well as expert obstetric consultation services provided by an outstanding local physician, Dr. Maurice Arons.

And just as she thought about Dr. Arons, there it was again—the pain, now sustained, and stronger.

Trying to steady her voice, she called for Clive. "Darling, could you come here for a moment?"

"Would you like y'r tea now, love?" Clive asked in his soothing Scottish burr.

"No. I'd very much like a word with you."

Clive was quickly out of the kitchen, drying his hands with the dishcloth, kneeling at her side. "What is it?"

She touched his face, his dark beard, salted with gray and trimmed short. She saw the fear rising in his clear gray eyes behind wire-rim spectacles. They'd been through this before.

"Any possibility it's just false labor?" he asked quietly, his hand on hers.

"I don't think so." She shook her head. "Too strong."

"How far are you along...thirty-two weeks?"

"Almost thirty-three—the furthest yet."

"It might be far enough—"

"I hope so."

Michael J Cooper writes historical fiction set in the Holy Land at major historical turning points and promoting coexistence. His books include *Foxes in the Vineyard* set in 1948, *Wages of Empire* set in 1914, and its sequel *Crossroads of Empire*. After high school, he emigrated to Israel and spent the next decade attending Hebrew University and Tel Aviv University Medical School. After graduating, he returned to the US to specialize in pediatric cardiology. After retirement, he continues to do volunteer missions serving Palestinian children who lack access to care. MichaelJCooper.net

Mother Earth

by Mimi Drop

Chapter 1: The Mother

White Mountains, California

Life is tenacious.

On the last living mountainside, Mother Tree crouches on a stony cliff as a hot wind whips up powdery white soil. As the gust wanes, she probes her curling branches for signs of distress. The temperature, for millennia an unchanging continuum from cold to warm to bearably hot, has reached a boil. But the smooth red surface of her trunk, no longer sheltered by bark, will withstand any challenge, and the gritty invasion of sand in her roots is nothing she can't correct, not yet.

The punishing conditions of her habitat have given a sculptural shape to her twisted limbs, bent them to resemble the wind itself. After decades of hardship, her branches are compromised, but her singular ability to adapt has kept her alive for thousands of years, perhaps tens of thousands. Small bundles of green pine needles shoot out and stand strong, short and densely grouped like the tassels on a queen's throne.

On this isolated peak, the trees have found sanctuary since time began. As the unnatural sun grew hotter, the trees grew higher up the mountain until they reached the top. Now there's nowhere left to go. Without snow and the great spring melt, water is so scarce the sage brushes are complaining.

A particularly gnarled branch is a welcoming perch for the golden eagle who lands there, overheated and exhausted. His beak noses into the folds of a wing and plucks out a mite, swallows it. Mother sends a greeting from her roots to the branch, one long pulse. The eagle settles his wings and squawks a reply. They continue this way with pulses, squawks, and wing taps conferring about the heat and the lack of water. The eagle flaps his wing against the tree's limb, "No squirrels. No lizards. All dying." He bobs his head. Mother reads the bird's fear through the clutch of his talons.

A rare gentle breeze caresses her needles and grants her a moment of relief. She opens her senses to the air that passes from tree to tree and communicates the dangers of bark beetles and drought, but on this day, there is no information at all. The eagle opens his wings to feel the breeze and resettles on the branch. Mother sends another pulse. "How many trees below?"

"Living trees? None."

Mother's senses go on alert. Without kin, her survival is at risk. She feels her way along the cliff with roots that wrap around rocks and stretch far down the mountain into the valley. She touches the root tip of many trees. None greet her. How can this be? Is she the last? If she, too, succumbs to the blistering sun her other children, the insects, birds, and fungi, will have no tree to support them. Without her, they will die.

Her mother and the many mother trees who preceded her dissolve into one long line of succession, each nurturing the next to adulthood, sharing a mycelial network, touching root to root. Her seed populated an entire mountain stretching to the next. No other trees competed for the land. Only they, the pines of White Mountain, could survive here. Until now.

She stretches her roots into the white dolomite soil that reflects the sun, cools the Earth, and anchors her to the pulsing life underground. Beneath her roots, the vast network of fungal threads, the mycelia, trades nutrients for sugar, the magical substance she creates from sunlight. She dips a loose root into the cluster. Still there, healthy, for now. But she doesn't sense ants or those pesky beetles. The hardiest creatures of all are struggling, disappearing. The balance of life hangs on a precipice. She needs to act. But how?

The vast system of branching mycelial threads runs miles underground and connects her to the world below. She pulses a message to the network, *Where are the humans?* When great changes take place, they are the most likely culprits. The mycelia report that a small human, a female as nimble as a ground squirrel, is climbing the mountain. She's passed the base and is on the second ridge.

Mother waits to see what damage the human will inflict. When she arrives at the top, the eagle glares at the woman in warning. She greets him with a gentle voice, "Look at you. My God, how magnificent." They lock eyes until the eagle cocks his head at an angle and preens. "And you," the human says to Mother, "alive and beautiful." The woman opens a plastic jug and pours water on Mother's roots, an offering. The water seeps in and cools Mother's trunk. Her needles quiver in gratitude.

"When I was a girl, I used to visit here. The trees were everywhere—as far as the next mountain and the next. And now…" She scrutinizes the dead wood descending into the valley and casts her gaze to the opposite peak. Her shoulders begin to shake. "How will we live without trees?" The human begins to weep wasting precious water, letting it evaporate without collecting it. She wraps her arms around the trunk and listens to the trickle of water making its way up. Mother sends a comforting pulse as the human presses herself against the bare wood and contemplates whatever unpractical thoughts are of human concern. Mother remembers her scent. As a girl, she was respectful, unlike many visitors.

The eagle with his permanent frown resettles on his branch. He appears to have grown sympathetic. When the sun reaches its noon fervor and heat begins to climb up the mountain, the woman appears to come to some conclusion. "Mother Tree, with luck I'll soon be gone from this planet and don't know if I'll ever return. You, of all the living things we've been so careless to destroy, must survive." She plucks a dried pinecone from the ground and squirrels it away in her pouch. With wet eyes, she takes one long look at Mother. The woman makes her way back down the mountain. It's a long climb.

Mother circulates the water through her resin canals and ruminates on the human's words. Leave the planet? Even in death, no creature leaves. Death provides life for another. Nutrients pass into a new generation and continue the cycle. Humans—such curious creatures.

A faraway rumble disturbs her musings. In a moment, it advances into a roar. The eagle screams and soars away, its wings gliding through the sky like a phantasm. The source of the disturbance, a giant human-made bird, streaks into view. With a screech of metal on metal, an opening appears in its rear. A cylinder thrusts through. Purple gas the color of a mature pinecone shoots out in great billowing circles. After a time, it gathers into a miles-long cloud.

The sky, forever an unchanging stratum from white to grey to blue, turns an unnatural hue, a gradation from purple to lavender. The cloud covers the sun and blocks the violent rays. The air turns cooler. Is this good or bad? It's the work of humans and that's never good.

There was a time when the free-floating creatures came to pay homage to Mother. With screaming vehicles, they built a path to her ledge increasing the chance of erosion to her roots. Some grunted their way up the mountain. A tall dark one bored a small hole straight through her and removed a long piece of her internal wood. She raced to fill the hole with resin and repair it, but that intrusion left a mark as obvious as everything they touched.

This one small female is the first Mother has seen in many moons. Did she summon the metal bird? For too long, the humans' spinning rubber feet erased the peacefulness of the valley bringing noise, pollution, and metal constructions they randomly planted. They disguised themselves in green, blue, or yellow coverings to look like flowers, a sinister practice, and filled the air with noxious smells, gases, and their own putrification. Now this.

In the weeks that follow, the cloud leaks a toxic substance instead of life-giving rain. The sky has sent hail and rigorous heat but never poison, not in all of Mother's long years. She releases a protective coating to her trunk and needles to armor them against the cloud droppings that smell like the odorous water humans leak. As Mother, it is her responsibility to clean the air, but she can't grow new needles without sunlight. And she can't clean the air alone, not with a danger this large.

Her limbs ache. The struggle to stay alive has exhausted her. Only one of her pinecones survives, one pinecone with one dormant seed. She has neither the strength nor the capability to make more. The cone has begun to mature and darken. Part of it has turned purple like the sky. To regain her family, she must give birth to a new Mother, younger and better able to reproduce. This seed is her last hope.

Mimi Drop's novel, *Mother Earth*, was a finalist in the Novel Slices contest and was longlisted in the *Masters Review* contest. Her fiction and poetry have been published in Flash Fiction Magazine, Bright Flash Literary Review, THAT Literary Review, So to Speak, The Woman in the Glass, and OnTheBus. Her commercial work has appeared in the New York Times, the Washington Post, Vogue Magazine, Harper's Bazaar, W Magazine, Allure, Vanity Fair, and dozens of television commercials. She lives in Los Angeles with a doting husband and a cranky old cat.

Effie & Avis

by Suzanne Johnson

Chapter 1: Double Trouble Cake
January, 1899 ~ Manhattan, NY

"Ma, do you think Frederick will come for my birthday?"

I ran my pinky finger down the side of the bowl for a taste of the creamed butter and sugar. Ma glanced from the bowl to my eyes. She was letting me know that both the question and my batter sampling were pushing the limits of her patience.

Don't ask me why I let that question slip out. I already knew the answer. My father would sooner fly to the moon than come home for my birthday. Sometimes I couldn't hold the devil in, even when Ma was baking a chocolate cake.

"What's gotten into you now?" Ma picked up the double boiler with the melted chocolate and milk, and lightly tapped the side of the pan. Too warm and it might ruin the egg yolks, too cool and it might not mix properly. She delicately dipped her own finger into the bowl and licked off the warm chocolate, giving me a sideways glance. "Hmm. Delicious."

Ma and I worked in silence for a while, practiced in the art of baking together. Chocolate cakes are a three-bowl process, and one of the few kitchen tasks worthy of extra dishwashing.

I held the largest bowl as Ma scraped gleaming chocolate into the mix. We swapped bowls so I could sift the flour and baking powder, ferociously squeezing the sifter handle while Ma folded the light-as-ash mixture into the batter.

Next came my favorite part: frothing the egg whites. I clamped the bowl to my ribs and whisked at a frantic pace, like a whirling dervish, as Ma said, til the egg whites foamed into snowy white peaks.

"But really. Do you think he might? I'm ten now, after all. That's a big deal."

Ma stepped back to consider me. I knew my eyes reminded her of Frederick, my father. Except his eyes flashed with gold specks while mine were more like mud pies, topped by eyebrows that would not stay still. If I lifted just one eyebrow I could make Ma smile. Just like my father used to do, until he left us.

In truth my father was a distant, mixed bag of memories. Sometimes I'd clamber up into his lap and he'd swing his legs around like a tot-sized roller coaster that made me holler and him laugh, a raspy guffaw like the bark of a big dog. Sawdust and smoke clung to his shirt and neck and I'd bury my face in it as long as he would tolerate that closeness.

We lived on West 18th in Manhattan, one flight of stairs up from father's street-level workshop. *Hotchkiss Boxes & Crates* read the window sign, and if you walked inside that was just what you'd find. All sizes of wooden boxes, some with straps and handles, some with hinged lids, some stamped with lettering. He made tool chests and travel trunks and potato crates. Tools hung over the workbenches at the back of the shop; planks and paint cans were stored below.

His workshop smelled of fresh cut pine with musky undertones of horse pee and leather, from when the space held a stable. Sawdust collected in the corners and soaked up the tobacco juice my father and the other men would spit onto the floor. Pine and leather and tobacco, a three-note cologne that will forever bring me back to the days I'd sit on the stairs, tucked out of sight, listening to him work.

The rhythmic rasp of a saw meant he was starting a new box. The quicker scratch of his files would follow, smoothing the rough wood. When he hammered the boards together, he pounded with such a fury I covered my ears, hard. Mostly I listened for his whistles.

On good days, he whistled bird calls—high clear notes and low trills like a blackbird, between bits of ragtime and church hymns. He could keep the songs going as he breathed in and out, like a harmonica. Sometimes outside the shop he'd cup his hands and blow between his thumbs to make a soft hollow hoot. Pigeons would land at his feet, bobbing their heads and peering up at him. I asked him to teach me and he just patted my head. So I practiced on the sly.

Some days he was quiet in the shop. I'd peek around the corner to see him staring at the walls like a man in a prison cell. But when customers jangled the bell on the door he'd shift back to smiling, back-slapping, smack-talking with the men who came in.

Mostly workmen in canvas aprons, sometimes pushcart vendors. Many with thick accents and little English. Father was quick to sketch out a design, quick with the numbers and measurements. Then they'd linger, cracking jokes and spitting tobacco juice into the sawdust. Only once did I see any ladies enter the Hotchkiss Boxes & Crates, and they did not come to place an order.

They came on a hot summer day when I was dawdling on the stairs, staying out of the heat. The three ladies leaned their bicycles against the shop window. Their straw hats were set at a jaunty angle, and their faces glowed with sweat and determination. They bustled through the doorway, arms filled with rolled-up posters and flyers.

"We represent the Ladies Health Protection Association," one woman trilled in a voice I knew my father would make fun of later. "As you may know, *expectoration* in public places causes the spread of disease, especially consumption. The sidewalks are drenched in sputum and sputum is full of germs. Will you help stamp out this epidemic by banning expectoration in your place of work?"

Right on cue, the two ladies behind her unfurled posters with anti-spitting slogans: *Beware the Careless Spitter!* and *No Spit = No consumption!* My father looked from one to the next, then turned his head and shot out a stream of brown tobacco juice into the corner. It was an admirable distance, even I could see that.

"Ladies," he greeted them with his most charming smile. "Of course. I surely will place that important information right where it will do the most good," he said, holding his hand out for the posters. He waited until they'd climbed back onto their bicycles before dropping it all into the trash bin. He didn't read the flyers, which listed the symptoms of consumption: exhaustion, night sweats, fever. Followed by chest pain, coughing, bloody phlegm, wasting away. Followed by death. Maybe he didn't want to know. Maybe he already knew what was brewing in his lungs.

As winter came on, consumption was everywhere—clean, spit-free sidewalks couldn't hold back the disease. People wore white masks over their faces; teachers moved our classrooms outside into fresh air. The slightest cough sparked panic in crowded apartments. The real name of this disease is tuberculosis, but consumption is so much more descriptive: the disease literally consumes its victims 'til they wither into nothing.

Over the winter we watched Father grow pale and gaunt. His trousers hung loose on his hips. The coughing fits made his back hunch over like an old man, the knobs of his spine poking through his shirt.

Ma cooked him bone broth and he'd glare as if this was all her fault. "There's not enough air in this city," he'd say. "I can't breathe here. You are suffocating me."

The windows stayed open at night to counter his fever sweats and left the rest of us to shiver. My baby brother Everett would snuggle with Ma in one bed, and I would spoon with my sister Avis in the other. Father slept on a daybed in the main room, propped up with pillows to help his breathing. All night we'd hear him grumble and gasp.

As winter waned Father grew restless, a change Ma took to show he was healing. On the first day of spring, he packed a small valise and hung a CLOSED sign in the window of his shop. The Loomis Sanatorium in the Catskills had a bed available, where the mountain air could restore him. Ma said it would be a lovely place for him to recuperate. We watched quietly as he prepared to leave us.

"I'll come once a month to visit. The children can stay with the neighbors," Ma offered.

"No visitors," he said, shaking his head sadly.

"I'm sure by summer you'll be fit as a fiddle!" Ma smiled hopefully.

Father locked the clasps on his valise and tucked the train ticket in his pocket.

With a hint of color in his cheeks and a little bounce to his step, Father nodded to Ma and patted us each on the head before setting off for the train station. Everett, Sister Avis, and I leaned into Ma as we watched his skinny back retreat into the crowded street.

I stopped calling him Father that day.

He was just Frederick now.

Suzanne Johnson is a midwest transplant who found home in the Cascade Mountains of Oregon. She has been a science teacher, an entrepreneur, and a beekeeper, with writing as the constant thread through it all. While much of her work is creative nonfiction, she is currently diving into the world of historical fiction, with a story that revolves around the lives of women adventuring through the American West. Find more of her writing at SuzanneMyhreJohnson.me.

The Messenger
by Jennifer Kennemer

Rachel gasped, surging upward from the dream like a diver running out of air, kicking and stretching toward the surface as the darkness closed in below. A series of panicked breaths followed as she heaved into a semi-state of awakened terror. *Where was she? Was she dead?*

It was not quite six a.m., and the light was dim. As her eyes adjusted, she began to pick out the familiar details of her room, including a set of decorative pillows now in a heap on the floor. *I'm home?*

Rachel felt her heart beating like a caged bird inside her chest and feared it might burst free. She whispered to it like a small child. *We're okay. We're okay. We're okay.* And practiced breathing techniques she learned from yoga at the local YMCA. With a hand pressed firmly over her untrustworthy heart, she looked out at her room and searched for any sign of the miraculous.

She saw her new church dress was draped over the back of a chair. It was lavender and very soft, and she remembered how it felt when she tried it on in the dressing room at the mall. The rare, perfect fit. How many people had complimented her last night at Bible study? The extra attention made her feel special and proud, even though it embarrassed her to celebrate such a silly success in her journal afterward.

She saw a series of camera lenses lined up and waiting to be cleaned; the different-sized, similarly-shaped containers reminded her of nesting dolls. Two weeks ago at the park, she was shooting pictures of a little girl she babysat, Annabel, when a windstorm took them by surprise. Bits of sand from the playground got between the polarizing filter and the lens and, with a little help, into the pockets of the little girl. Enough to start an indoor beach, the mother had told her over the phone.

She saw the Bible sitting closed on the bedside table. The sticky notes protruding from its pages reminded her of teeth. Rachel turned on the lamp and reached out to touch the familiar leather cover. Her small brown hand hesitated, hovering midair. *Please,* she prayed, *please let it be a dream.*

The Bible was a birthday gift from her father. A good man, she thought. Not as stern or remote as some other fathers. He'd inscribed a message on the inside flap about growing in faith and growing into a magnificent young woman. The book had been meticulously wrapped in delicate pink paper with a white lace bow. Rachel believed that no daughter had ever received such a beautiful gift from their father. She folded the pink paper and tucked it into the back of the Bible, the ribbon she saved for her wedding day.

The paper, when she checked with shaking hands, was still there. The message, as familiar to her as many of the verses, was also there. She traced the cursive letters with her fingers and sighed.

Just a dream then.

Rachel pushed back the blanket and swung her feet toward the ground, her toes brushing against a pair of fuzzy slippers. Silly, shaped like the head of a unicorn, Rachel had discovered them during a shopping trip with her mother before her senior year. She loved them instantly, with every ounce of child that remained inside her, but at seventeen, she knew they weren't cool or sexy. The joy of them eventually won out, and she'd smuggled them into the cart and hid them under a sweater, swearing a silent oath that no one other than her parents would ever see her wearing them.

Yet God loved her, and probably unicorns, too.

It was a habit to slip them on, so she did, moving to sit at her ornate, wooden vanity. Once seated, Rachel was almost hesitant to look in the mirror as the dream tugged insistently at her again. In some ways, it felt no less real than the memory of the shopping trip despite the utter strangeness of it all.

Rachel had heard God's voice in her dream, or at least, she thought she had. The dream itself started as a pleasant walk through a fantastical garden, the likes of which she had never seen — not even on Instagram. There was such an abundance of colorful, sweet-smelling flowers that it soon overwhelmed her system. Later, Rachel told her best friend it was like standing at the perfume counter at the mall; it hurt her head. Then, she started to sneeze violently and rapidly. Bracing herself against a stone archway, she reached up to her nose and came away with an awful mixture of snot and blood.

Rachel ran into a wooded area with tall, leafless trees just beyond the garden. It looked like there were faces in the fat, gnarled trunks, and she felt watched, even hunted, as the forest grew thick and dense around her. A branch cut her face, and she cried out, but no one else came, and Rachel knew she was lost.

Rachel never felt more cold and unsettled as the sun disappeared from the sky. She followed the path into the heart of the woods and spotted a cave. No stars were visible to guide her, and she had no plan to get home. A power beckoned from inside the cave. An invisible hand seemed to propel her, and she followed, crawling on her hands and knees when the walls grew close. It was not unlike a coffin, and she feared the earth would swallow her up, but the presence, the very rock itself, seemed to call her forward into the cavern.

It was in this cavern that she heard the voice of God. She experienced the voice of God. It did more than fill her mind; it filled her body, lighting a fire from within that pushed out the cold. She forgot what cold meant. There was only a steady, throbbing warmth and the voice.

She knelt in supplication and dared not search for the source of the voice. It seemed to emanate most strongly from the rock formation in front of her, a complicated mass of stalagmites and stalactites not unlike a cancer cell she studied in biology class.

The voice said, *child, know that I am God, the one true God, and heed my word, for I am in need of a messenger.*

Lord, she replied, *I'm just a girl.*

Yes. But thou art humble and true.

Rachel pulled back from the dream and returned to her current dilemma.

Hadn't Moses turned into Santa Claus after looking upon the burning bush? Rachel was grateful there was no bush in her dream, even as she wondered if hearing the voice of God would be enough to line her face like a wrinkled shirt. She imagined her brown skin surrounded by a shock of white hair like her nana Rosemary and felt equal parts fear and guilt.

Worrying about her appearance was the height of vanity and sin. If she truly heard the voice of God, youth would seem a small sacrifice, but was it one she was ready to face?

She looked.

Her mirror showed her regular appearance: big, brown eyes set in an oval face with long black hair peeking out from a colorful scarf. It usually had a kinky texture, her hair. Her mother had let her straighten it at a salon for graduation. The bright red scarf made her think about her bloody nose in the dream. Queasy, she pulled it loose and set it on the vanity. There was no scratch on her face. No sign that she had been blessed by the divine.

Relieved, Rachel studied her face and accepted that she was what people considered pretty but not beautiful. Her body was lean and muscular because her parents encouraged her to try for the high school track team. A long distance runner, not a sprinter. She was smart but not a genius, certainly not in math. Maybe it was silly to think that God would speak to someone so average.

Even in the dream, telling God no one would listen to her seemed impertinent. The girl sitting here was no leader, no shepherd. She was a member of the flock. It embarrassed her that her voice shook when she read aloud passages from the Bible during services. Didn't God need someone with a strong voice?

Oh no, she thought, *what if it had been Satan?*

Jennifer Kennemer is a veteran and public affairs instructor who also writes fiction that explores how modern issues intersect with everyday lives. You can connect with her on LinkedIn.

The Meaning of Eli

by Tracy Sand

He stood at a distance from the group of mourners. By then he was rail thin, dressed in black, in a large wool overcoat. The day was wet. The fog thick and low enough for one of his favorite lines: "The great thing about being in San Francisco is you can't tell you're in San Francisco."

He had no idea she was there.

Every funeral has a ghost, but not always the ghost you expect.

TAPE DIARY PRELUDE, Cate and I First Meet: Monday, November 23, 1992

Dr. Andre Gilligan told me my cancer is back, and I have about five months to live. Aside from this news, it's been a good morning.

I'm in the lobby of Piedmont Hospital, looking to join a terminal illness support group.

The desk clerk's nametag reads *Bette*. "Our support group is at capacity."

"Oh."

"We formed another group for people who couldn't get into that one."

"Terrific."

"Unfortunately, that group is now at capacity."

"It's an excellent time of year to die."

I can tell she disapproves of my levity. Death shouldn't be funny. Especially if you're the person it's happening to.

"Is there a waitlist?"

"A wait list?"

"People must leave these groups on a, um, regular basis."

"I wish I could help."

"No, you don't."

"Sir," she says firmly. I love it when people call me sir. It makes me feel like a maitre d'. As a poet and professor, I usually don't get that kind of respect. I'm pudgy, too. You'd think my errant black hair and bad boy looks would compensate. You'd think that, and you'd be wrong.

Bette is still talking. "Find a hospital whose group has openings."

"That's the peculiar thing. My oncologist called around. He does everything possible to help people. You know anyone like that?"

I'm waiting for Bette to understand what I'm really saying. Her face flushes.

"Did it get hotter in here?" I ask innocently. "Every support group Dr. Gilligan checked in the East Bay was full. Someone at Piedmont Hospital said the computer was down, but they were sure there was an opening. Dr. Gilligan told me to head on over."

"Whomever he spoke with was wrong."

"She told him her name was Bette."

Bette doesn't appear the least bit sorry, then says, "I'm sorry."

When she says this, I realize she is in her sixties, at least twenty years older than I am, and that I will never reach her age. I will never even approach it. I flinch a little, tell myself things could be worse. How, I don't know. I guess I could already be dead.

The hospital lobby holds a faint odor of disinfectant. Somewhere someone is killing germs. This doesn't reassure me. Kill all the germs you want, you're still all going to die, I want to warn everyone.

Instead, I focus on Bette, in her silk dress with black-and-white squares. If she were less threatening, she could be a chessboard. She claps her hands. I leap a little. These are moments I'll never get back, and I'm spending them with Bette.

"Gotcha," she says, tapping away at her computer. "There's a group in Redwood City."

"That's more than an hour-and-a-quarter drive."

"On the way to it you can practice what you're going to talk about."

"I'm not joining a support group to make a sales pitch. I'm looking for someone who empathizes with an impossible situation."

"What situation?"

"Becoming a dead guy."

Poor Bette looks like she's trying to swallow a basketball. To her credit, she musters her forces and delivers a withering stare. I want to respond appropriately, so I ring the bell in front of her.

"What are you doing?" she asks.

"Calling someone to help."

"That someone is supposed to be me."

"You said it, I didn't. Why don't you give me the contact info for the people leading the two support groups here?"

"It's the same person," she says, as though this ends the discussion.

"Then it should take you less time to give me that info."

"*Sir*, why don't you want to go to Redwood City? Do you feel driving is bad for the environment?"

"Driving *is* bad for the environment. But right now, I'm concerned about having a limited time in this world and spending more than two-and-a-half hours of it each week going to Redwood City."

"What do you have against Redwood City?"

I take a breath. I pace in front of her counter and lift my arms. If I was outside, I'd be invoking the heavens. Instead, I'm invoking a low 1960s corkboard ceiling. "I HAVE NOTHING AGAINST REDWOOD CITY."

I'm surprised I haven't attracted a security guard. Maybe no one loses their shit in Piedmont.

Bette doesn't look the least bit worried. In fact, she seems pleased with my reaction. She nods.

I question her sanity. Then mine. Then the sanity of the person who hired her.

I decide to cut my losses. I need to get away from her. Regroup.

I sit in a chair along the wall of the lobby, catching my breath. The disinfectant is stronger, a pine scent. I'm ten feet from Bette, you would think far enough away.

Until she says, "Those chairs are for patients and their families."

I gaze at her in disbelief.

"You don't appear ill."

On my list of favorite events today, I can now add, *Accused of fake dying*. "Please leave me alone."

"But surely that must be good."

"It isn't, and stop calling me Shirley."

"You can fill out a complaint form, Sir. Even about me." She points to a small wooden box on the counter with paper and red pencil stubs next to it.

I'm tempted, I really am. I start to get up, but a thought stops me. "Who handles the complaint forms?"

She looks weary. "I do. If you fill it out, I *will* read it."

"Then you'll get rid of it."

She grimaces. "In your case, certainly, Sir."

The front door opens with a puff of cold air. A woman in a trench coat walks in. Click, click on the linoleum floor. She disappears.

Bette eyes me. I eye her back. We seem to have reached an agreement. We agree I'm having a breakdown.

"You can't sit there, Sir."

I don't respond.

"Shouldn't you be at work?"

"I called and rearranged my schedule for the support group, I teach English Literature."

"My father was a professor of English."

"I'm a poet."

Now Bette becomes unnaturally silent and nods understandingly. This makes me feel the worst I've felt all morning. I tell myself to cheer up, I won't be a poet much longer.

It's strange how someone you don't know, whom you dislike, suddenly sees you more clearly than people you've been around for years.

The trench coat woman returns. "I'm lost. Can either of you help?"

I point both index fingers at Bette. The trench coat woman stares, but goes to the counter to whisper to her.

And like that, I've rid myself of the information desk clerk from hell. But I'm more alone than ever, with no support group. Desolation fills my gut and I sink deeper in my chair. It is burgundy plush, with a folding bottom like in a movie theater. If my life flashes before me when I die, I want to be in a chair like this with a box of popcorn.

I tell myself to act with the gravitas appropriate to a dying person.

It doesn't work. It doesn't seem like I'm going to die. It really doesn't. I'm just more tired than usual.

I close my eyes for I don't know how long. I understand how depression means a hole.

#

I'm jolted from this by what sounds like a thirteen-year-old girl yelling.

"I MAY WORK HERE, BUT THAT DOESN'T MEAN I HAVE TO HELP!"

To my horror, it is Bette, who appears to be reciting her life philosophy. She's jabbing her finger at the computer for the woman in the trench coat. "See! Both have twenty people. That's five over the maximum number. In each one. I don't make the rules. I do my job and earn my paycheck, lady."

The woman in the trench coat puts her hands on her hips. "You might be getting paid. But you aren't doing your job."

I suppress the urge to clap.

"I found you another group with four openings in Redwood City."

"Do you know how exhausting it is to drive to Redwood City?"

I'm beginning to question the customer satisfaction levels at Piedmont Hospital.

Bette points at me. "He's sick, too, and as rude as you are. Why don't you form a support group with *him?*"

The woman in the trench coat looks over. "Sorry about this. I'm Cate."

Tracy Sand is an award-winning playwright under the name Simon Fill. He is the recipient of a Yaddo Fellowship. He can be reached at SimonFill@aol.com

Road to Damascus

by Esther St. James

"Me uamá," my companion introduced me. I did not understand what it meant and took a quick glance around. The cabin furnishings were scarce. Two sleeping mats, a low table and four tiny three-legged stools. A steaming clay pot stood on the table. The smell of the food was divine

The woman pulled a stool into the corner and gesticulated for me to sit, while she and her grandson ate their dinner.

After the meal, the woman bent her finger inviting me to come closer. She asked something in her guttural tongue and my companion translated: *"Has matado a alguien?"*

I abhor violence, and recent experiences fortified that aversion. I opened my mouth to pronounce a resounding 'no', but then paused. The woman just learned that her grandson met me in prison. Perhaps her question was not as offensive as I initially thought. More importantly I could not answer with certainty. Someone could have died because of my blunder.

"Not willingly…" I tried to be truthful. She nodded and sent her grandson away.

For the next few hours, we sat in complete silence, as the sun slowly descended. My hunger became unbearable. I pointed a finger to my mouth and made chewing noises. My hostess pointedly ignored me.

What kind of backassward hospitality was practiced here?

When it became dark, the woman lit a candle in front of a small figurine I hadn't noticed earlier. The flickering light distorted the view making the sculpture indiscernible. A jaguar? A bear? Do bears live here? A capybara? I could not be certain.

The woman left the hut and returned with another clay vessel. She filled a carved wooden cup and sipped staring at me. Then she filled it again, made hissing noises and pushed the cup into my hand.

The concoction had an unusual color resembling glowing amber, dark red with an oily surface. A feeling of terror rippled through me, but the emotion was fleeting, and I gulped the liquid. Not an easy task. The brew was as viscous as olive oil and tasted of bark. I struggled through half and pushed the cup away. My hostess pointed angry finger, forcing me to finish the drink.

We waited. She, smoking her cigar, I, gagging over the putrid taste on my tongue. Finally, I lost my patience and deciding to end this travesty of a medical procedure, got up. My legs buckled and I fell with a moan, realizing that the surroundings had changed.

The air took on a three-dimensional quality, shimmering and flickering. It reminded me of the Cathedrale Notre Dame de Chartres. As if the stained glass illuminated by the sun twirled in a stunning display. This vision persisted for a while, though I cannot be sure for how long. Time itself took on a different connotation.

The walls disappeared. I saw jungles: lizards, birds and rodents rushed towards the hut to take a closer look at me. I understood their curiosity, they'd never seen a white man. A fluorescent frog jumped onto my chest and stared into my eyes. Occasionally her bright orange tongue reached out and touched my lips. It felt comforting.

I heard an odd noise and with some effort realized that my hostess was singing. It was an odd song, but it brought me back to reality. Reality is a wrong word. It thrust me not back, but forward, into an alternate dimension.

My hostess had an unusual voice, melodious and gravelly at the same time. The song had no accompaniment except for a sound that reminded me of a raindrop pitter. It emanated from the necklace the woman wore. Made from nut shells, it rattled every time she moved. All the animals fled as soon as they heard the ratchet.

Warmth arose in my chest and spread through my entire body. It was not a physical sensation, more an emotional swell. An upsurge of love. Love I was not familiar with. Not a filial love nor the love for God or one's country, not an erotic love, not a brotherly love…it was a boundless, all-inclusive love. An absolute love I did not know existed. A love that changes everything. A love that fills one's life with meaning.

Despite my effort to cling to that feeling, the sensation began slipping away, leaving me devastated. Tears rolled down my face. I knew I'd never experience anything so momentous for the rest of my life. Though I could attain it in death. The awareness was so profound I collapsed to the floor.

That moment I saw my hostess. She appeared huge, her massive torso and colossal breasts draped in a shiny wrap. Her face was covered by a crudely carved mask with mouth agape. Through the holes I saw her dark eyes, lit from inside with an otherworldly, black light. Above the mask sat a headgear of flowers and bird feathers. The moment I saw her in all her splendor the song ended, and I was hurled back into the darkness.

The next few minutes were filled with terror. The terror that made my previous anguish seem trivial. I realized how insignificant I was. An ant staring at Everest would feel giant compared to me. My ambitions were reduced to dust and my world imploded.

I was no longer in the Amazonian hut. I was in a small house I've never seen before. Whitewashed walls with exposed logs, two narrow beds, a dilapidated table. This new vision did not frighten me. By then, I'd lost my capacity to be startled.

I detected a movement and saw that one bed was occupied. An old man looked at me disapprovingly. I've never seen him before, yet he looked familiar. A few minutes passed in silence as we gauged each other.

"You're a despicable, graceless scoundrel. I am ashamed of you." The old man's revulsion was so intense I screamed. Sharp pain overwhelmed me. It felt as if an arrow pierced me. Right through the heart. I realized I'd wasted my life, and I was… well, exactly as he said… a wicked, rotten villain.

Oh, my God, how did I become such a person?

I knew the rights from the wrongs, and yet I allowed my life to become a sham. I betrayed my family. And for what? For a cruel stranger to think favorably of me? For that I adhered to a ridiculous criminal code?

Why?! For money? Out of fear? To fit in?

The arrow lodged in my chest turned white-hot. The pain became so intense I lost my ability to respond, even though the old man and I communicated in a mysterious telepathic way. Only gurgles emanated from my extrasensory facility, identical to the noises from my mute mouth. Thrashing on the floor, I stretched my hand hoping that the man would notice. He waved dismissively and sunk into his pillow.

I don't know how long I writhed in agony. Every time I thought the pain was subsiding, it returned even more intensely. My torture at the hands of the Uruguayan police felt now like a pleasant conversation. As my mind was about to crack, I heard a quiet melody.

What a relief it was to know that my *curandera* was still there. I simply cannot express the love I felt for her. For the first time since my mother's mysterious vanishing, I relinquished control, allowing my mind to drift.

I closed my eyes, and the pain diminished. Albeit slowly. I was back in the hut and a now familiar Charrua doctress sat on a low stool next to me. She reverted to her normal appearance, a long dress, and sandals. Did I see compassion in her eyes? I don't know. She placed her hand on my burning chest. I felt the remnants of the pain transferring into her palm. I saw my body from above. A bright light filled my form except for a reddish knot in my throat. My hostess moved her arm, and the lump dissolved.

I saw the first rays of the sun penetrating through the lattice-like walls. And then I fell asleep. Or perhaps lost consciousness.

When I came about the sun was in zenith. My companion sat on the floor, staring at me. He helped me up and poured some water on my hands and face. We shared a bowl of fish stew. It was the most delicious meal I've ever had.

I asked him what kind of fish it was without realizing that I spoke for the first time in seven years. My mutism was gone. My host chuckled. And I laughed with him.

After the meal, I searched for the *curandera* to express my gratitude, but she was nowhere to be found.

We boarded the dinghy and rowed to the township. I boarded a flatboat that was sailing to Nueva Palmira. The moment I saw my companion waving at me, I realized I did not know his name. How embarrassing…but it was too late. The rushing waters separated me and him forever.

Esther St. James (1922-2016) is the author of *Road to Damascus*. Regretfully, very little is known about her life. A refugee arriving in the US in the mid-1930s, she was reclusive and fiercely private. All her life she attempted to follow the credo introduced by her parents: "Say what you know, do what you must, and come what may." Her entire career was dedicated to books and book lovers and for over 50 years she served as a librarian at the Salt Lake Public Library.

Spirits of the Grand Palace
by Giselle Stancic

Chapter 1: A thousand years ago

Stars danced across the mountain peaks, guiding the teenage girl as she crept through the gnarled brush. The rocks on the hillside cut through her soft moccasins and the north wind chilled her to the bone. Her long black hair kept getting caught on the brambles, slowing down her escape.

The shouting of the men grew fainter. Turning off the trail worked, but not for long. They would return to find her, unless she could make it to the cave first.

To calm herself, she patted the leather pouch on her right hip. Inside lay her people's sacred treasure, given to her by the Elder to protect when the raiders attacked their village. Wevo was the fastest runner, and she knew the way to the cave.

"Wait in the Great Room," he told her. "We will come for you."

Loud voices again pierced the still of the night.

"*Mokwic, mokwic!*"

Wevo gritted her teeth. *Why do they call us "small people" when our men are tall and brave?*

But she couldn't waste time being angry. She scrambled forward, yet in her hurry she slipped and tumbled down on her left leg. She felt a snap, followed by a shot of searing pain. She dared not cry out.

With the men closing in on her, she crawled the rest of the way. She moved aside the branches hiding the narrow entrance. She lowered herself into the tunnel like her father had shown her. On her good leg, she perched on the rope ladder dangling down to the cave. She reached up to draw the branches back into place as best as she could.

She hobbled down the ladder on one leg until she dropped to the bottom. This time she couldn't deny her shrieks of pain. She grabbed her left shin and felt something hard and wet. Above her the men yelled and stomped, until at last the earth became quiet again. Wevo was alone, in pitch black, deep under the ground.

She groped around the cave floor until she found a pine torch left behind by an earlier visitor. She reached into her leather pouch, taking care not to disturb the carved clay figures of a man and a woman, nestled in their deerskin wrapping. She took out a small piece of flint from the bag and began striking it against the limestone wall. Sparks flickered, and she held the torch close until the frayed end started to smolder.

Once the flame took hold, she held the torch above her left leg. She closed her eyes to keep from fainting. Below her knee, a jagged bone pierced through the torn, bloody skin.

Minutes passed before she could look again. She had to bind the wound to keep going. She tore off the bottom of her woven skirt and wrapped it tightly around the protruding fracture. She gave in to the agony for a few seconds. Then she clawed on the walls to get up to her feet.

Wevo gave a silent offering to her ancestors buried in the cave, asking for their protection. Surrounded by their spirits, she used the flickering torch light to follow the drawings on the walls, leading her through the spider web of chambers. She wriggled through the tightest sections of the maze, sometimes on her hands and knees, reinjuring her leg again and again. The air was dank and sour smelling, making it hard to breathe.

After more turns and twists, she realized she was lost. But she couldn't go back, she didn't have the strength. She forced herself forward a few more steps, around the next outcropping. Her hand cradled the leather pouch, keeping the carvings close to her. She peered past the rocks and her heart sank. More of the same. But just as she was about to give up, a faint drawing of a man caught her eye.

Keep going.

She limped along, moving on instinct. The dusty cave trail turned into a slick wet surface. She was near water, and where there was water...

Suddenly the Great Room opened in front of her. Giant rocks dripped down from the soaring ceilings, and spectacular formations erupted through the floor around her. Glorious, ribbed bands in the stone, pinks, reds, and browns, marked the passage of eons of time and rivers of flowing water. She had been here after her grandmother's passing, and she'd never forgotten the feeling of being in such an otherworldly place.

"Wait in the Great Room. We will come for you."

Finally, she could sigh with relief.

She picked her way down the rocky path to the shimmering pool of water on the far side of the cavern. She lay down on the craggy ledge, her hand grazing the cool water. The wrapping around her leg oozed with blood. Her foot below was numb.

She dozed off, only to be jolted awake by shouts echoing through the cave.

"*Mokwic, mokwic!*"

With her heart pounding, she stared at the dark crevice past the pool. Evil spirits lived in the black caves beyond the Great Room. No one was allowed to enter. But if she stayed here, she would suffer a fate worse than death, and her tribe's memory would be lost forever. They were depending on her.

Wevo tried to stand but her good leg wouldn't hold her. So, she dragged herself into the forbidden abyss. She snuffed out the torch. She would have to feel her way over the rocks. Even if the raiders figured out where she'd gone, they would be too afraid to follow.

She would be on her own, until...

Chapter 2: A thousand years later

"Are we there yet?"

Louise leaned her head against the passenger side window. Bob gazed through the windshield at the endless two-lane highway stretched out ahead of them through the sun-swept Nevada desert.

"Just a little longer, dear," he said.

She rolled her eyes. "You said that an hour ago."

After retiring, volunteering at a national park was at the top of both of their bucket lists. Bob suggested Great Basin because the Lehman Caves reminded him of boyhood adventures. Louise got excited about the Fremont culture pictographs on the cave walls. Still, maybe they should have volunteered for a park in more lush surroundings. Hawaii was on the list, too. But they were here now and would have to make the best of it, together.

At last, the sign for the visitor center appeared. Wheeler Peak loomed before them over a thankfully greener landscape. After Bob parked the car, Louise made a beeline for the restrooms.

"Nature calls," she said. "You go ahead."

In the center, a young man behind the information desk talked with a couple of student backpackers. Bob checked the brochures until they were finished.

"Good morning, Sir. Are you looking for our seniors' guide to the park?"

Bob bristled at the age reminder but held back a prickly response.

"Good morning," he said, with a smile. "My wife and I are here for volunteer orientation. Bob and Louise Pepper."

"Oh, sorry about that." The young man chuckled. "I'm Ranger Chris. You're a little early, but you folks can check out the exhibits until we get started."

One of the backpackers motioned for the ranger to come back over.

"Excuse me," he said.

Louise joined Bob at the desert plants display. She was back to her usual cheerful self. There were only a few wisps of gray in her light brown hair, and she'd kept the trim figure of her youth. What she saw in him, a balding guy with extra around the middle, Bob couldn't imagine. But she'd stuck with him all these years.

She slipped her hand into his. "Find out anything?"

"We're the oldest ones here."

As they spoke, another park ranger walked into the center. She had dark eyes and her black hair was pulled back in a long braid. She spoke with Chris, then they looked over at Bob and Louise.

"She's coming this way," whispered Louise.

"Hi, Mr. and Mrs. Pepper. I'm Ranger Tassie." She pointed to the badge on her lapel, which read "Tasela Yazzie."

"I'm supposed to do your orientation, but they need me up at the caves."

Bob's heart jumped. They were already talking about the caves.

The ranger studied them for a moment. "You're wearing hiking boots."

"We wanted to be ready," said Louise.

"Our seniors always come prepared," said Ranger Tassie.

Bob let the comment pass. What about the caves?

"Hmm, you're supposed to watch the first aid video," the ranger said.

Louise squeezed Bob's hand.

"We're both certified for CPR." She was up to something.

"Normally we wouldn't do this, but we're so short-handed," said Ranger Tassie. "Would you folks be interested in going on the Grand Palace cave tour with me? To help me keep the group moving. I know you just got here, but if you're not too tired…"

Bob and Louise glanced at each other. They answered, together.

"Absolutely."

Giselle Stancic is a San Francisco Bay Area writer who draws upon her classical music background to give voice to the untold stories of musical performers on and off the stage. Find out more at MusicMysteries.com.

The Circle of Grace

by Merry Zavala

September 8, 1900 — Gonzales Texas

"I smell a storm," Mother muttered. "Rain's a'coming; my knee has been hurting somethin' awful. Ruth, Suzanna, get down from that tree." She held a clutch of eggs in her apron from the coop behind the diner. "We need to go home and make some victuals in case we get laid up a spell." It was uncanny how Mother's knee only hurt when it was going to rain.

That morning, we played in the ancient oak in our fort high among the leaves that shadowed the front of Mother and Father's diner, The Cattle Horn, named for the massive set of Texas longhorns that hung over the front window.

"Come on, girls," Mother called up to us again. "Get down from there."

I jumped from the ladder and glanced up at the morning clouds, unimpressed by the look of them. Sure didn't look like rain to me.

Mother turned the sign on the blue door of the diner from "open" to "closed," handing my sister Suzanna the basket of eggs. Then she leaned down to collect a passel of fresh vegetables and supplies left on the porch. "Ruth, bring along the apples, will ya?" she asked.

I bit into an apple and passed one to my sister. The juice ran down my chin.

"Where's Father?" I asked between several big bites.

"He's nailing some boards over the windows and locking up."

"Why don't we stay at the diner?" I asked, tossing the core into the brush and wiping my chin with my apron.

"We're too close to the river here," Mother said.

We traipsed the quarter mile up the road to the house. Once home, we started a pot of chili bean, mixed some biscuits, and brought jars of food up from the cellar to have at the ready. Mother wrinkled her brow and mumbled, as she filled the lanterns and stuffed rags around the edges of the door and windows. She asked Suzanna to bring in a clean night pot and washbasin from outside. All the while, I stirred the chili.

"Those beans sure smell good," Mother said. "I'm glad you're not letting them burn."

Father's booming voice filled the room as he opened the kitchen door a crack, "We better make haste; it'll be raining bullfrogs by tonight. I'm goin' out to take care of the livestock." The door slammed behind him.

Late afternoon, ominous dark and gloomy clouds filled the sky. We gulped our dinner and cleaned up. Rain started softly, and the air was oppressive, humid, and quiet as a graveyard. We huddled in the drawing room. Mother's chair creaked while she rocked, knitting a baby blanket for the poor box at church. Father sat on the horsehair sofa and nervously twiddled his thumbs. The pages of his almanac lay open beside him, but he hadn't glanced at it. Suzanna and I sat at the table sorting an enormous pile of pinto beans, separating them from the pebbles and debris.

We finished our chore by filling a large crock with the beans, and I gathered the bits of stone and dirt in my apron. I opened the door unthinkingly and threw out the chaff, which immediately blew back into my face. I slammed the door, replacing the rags. Glancing at Suzanna, she rolled her eyes.

"Let's sleep in here tonight," Mother said.

We helped her gather the blankets from the rooms and made the shakedown beds. The great room turned dusky, and Father lit the lamp. We huddled in the middle, a shudder of excitement and fear smote my back upon hearing the commotion outside.

The lantern flickered, and wind whispered through cracks in the drafty house. We heard branches scratch the walls, and the weather battered the windows. Raindrops pattered like rats square dancing on the shingled roof.

"Mother, can we keep the lamp lighted?" I asked.

"Yes, I suppose so." She said, tucking us in and giving us a kiss. "Say your prayers. You'll see everything is gonna be alright. I've been through much worse than this."

I swallowed my doubt.

The gusts of wind howled through the enormous old oak trees like hundreds of little devils shrieking and whistling. An occasional downpour thwacked the house with fury. Frightened and uneasy, I sank deeper into the bedding, rolling myself into a ball. I closed my eyes, but sleep was slippery. Eventually, I heard slow, even breathing coming from Mother and Father's side of our makeshift bed, easing my fears. Still, I tossed and turned, landing squarely eye-to-eye with my dolly, Josie.

My mother had made Josie from homespun and dressed her in a blouse and skirt made of linsey-woolsey. She'd used some of Father's dark curly hair to make a wig.

Where's Sally? Where's Suzanna's doll? I crawled out from underneath the covers and tiptoed into our bedroom. I couldn't find her. Sally wasn't in the kitchen or anywhere in the house. I laid down next to Suzanna and poked her side until she stirred.

"Where's Sally?" I whispered.

Sally was quite magical, and I envied my sister's beautiful doll. Auntie Caroline, who left Texas to visit family in Europe, brought Suzanna's Sally all the way over from Germany.

"I don't know," she mumbled sleepily, turning over.

I shook her shoulder. "Wake up. I've looked everywhere. I can't find her."

Sally's big blue eyes opened when she was upright and closed when she lay down. Her long chestnut-colored hair was like mine, and she had rosy cheeks on a porcelain bisque face. Sally's soft body was hand-sewn in linen and she wore an ivory silk dress. I loved the flower tacked onto a pink ribbon that decorated her hair.

Now wide awake, Suzanna said, "I must have left her up in the tree when Mother called us down this morning."

I gasped in horror and whispered, "We can't leave her out there in the storm!"

I gently crept from underneath the crazy patch quilt that covered us.

Suzanna sputtered, "Wh...wh...where are you going?"

"I need to go to the privy."

"Remember, I put the bedpan over there in the corner," she said. "We don't need to go out."

"Come on! We've got to get Sally," I whispered urgently. "She might get blown away or, worse yet, swept down the river. I just gotta save her!"

"Oh, Ruth, I don't know. I don't want to get in trouble," Suzanna said.

"But it's... it's Sally, come on," I insisted.

"You're braver than me." She heaved a sigh and said, "Okay, okay, I can't let you go alone."

The door creaked as we unlocked it. We pulled on our coats and looked to where Mother and Father slept. They didn't stir. Suzanna was right behind me when we stepped out into the pelting rain. With our heads down, we fought the wind. I grabbed Suzanna's hand lest we be swept away. We ran down the path by the railroad tracks, soon wading in big puddles.

Suzanna yelled, "We should go back; the river's rising."

"You go on," I hollered. "I'll get Sally and come straight home."

"No, Ruth, it's too dangerous." Suzanna was always the practical one. "Leave it, come on, let's go home."

I dropped Suzanna's hand and rushed forward, intent on my mission. That was the last time I saw her that night, sloshing through the swirling, muddy current after me.

The sound of the tempest assaulted my ears, and darkness masked the landscape. The wind pushed hard on my back like a ghost opening a coffin. I squinted into the storm. A black shape rushed towards me. I feared it was the reaper from Father's story he told us last summer. Suddenly, my feet lifted off the ground. I screamed and fought away certain death.

"Settle down, Ruth. I'm right here," Father yelled into my ear. "Where's your sister?"

"I don't..." I said, throwing my arms around his neck. "I don't know. She was back there." I cried and pointed from where I came.

"Your mother is at the diner!" he shouted. "She'll get you home." Holding me with one arm, he raised the other out straight as if he was attempting to push the weather back. I was crushed against his chest. Water lapped at the bottom step of the diner's back stoop. Mother opened the door and hugged us.

"I'm gonna find Suzanna," Father said. He set back out into the relentless wind.

The door creaked. Mother grasped at the knob to close it, but it slipped from her hands and opened wide. The twists and turns of the storm ripped it off its hinges, and the single lightbulb in the kitchen swung wildly on its cord.

"Come on, Ruth. Let's get home." Mother determinedly grabbed my hand and pushed me out into the cyclone; every step forward was a challenge. An occasional flash of lightning frightened away the darkness. We strained to see our path forward. I wept, getting farther and farther away from Father and where Suzanna surely must be.

Merry Zavala enjoys living in Northern California and spending time with her family. *Circle of Grace* is a love letter to Ms. Zavala's mother's Southern heritage, a family saga spanning fifty years, following the lives of three strong women and exploring themes of resilience, love, and the enduring power of family ties. Ms. Zavala's journey is marked by a love of reading, immersion in Mexican culture, and a career in healthcare, which have instilled in her a deep appreciation for human connection and the power of storytelling. Find her on LinkedIn, Facebook, or Instagram.

Adult Nonfiction

Category Winner

On Dating & Job-Searching

By Chrisie Clark

I've come to the realization that dating closely mirrors the emotional turmoil of finding a job. As a single, 35-year-old woman (no pronouns, pls) fresh off completing a master's degree in real estate development (ahem*) amid a backdrop of living abroad in Madrid – BEST LIFE DECISION THUS FAR – I've entered a unique, albeit familiar, stage of transitioning (*"be careful how you use that word," mom says*). I now find myself in the position of wanting. I want a job. And I want a partner.

As a result of all this wanting, I am constantly questioning which style of communication is best. How much time do I spend A/B testing approaches, check ins, cold-emailing, texting, just plain calling, and waiting. What are the best strategies for a successful outcome in both areas?

Examples of questions to consider:

DATING:

• Do I commit to the cause fully, and saturate my presence online by paying subscription/services + fees for ALL dating apps?

• Does Tinder hold the same connotation in the US as it did in Spain where it was the most popular app – or does it mean just a hook up?

• Am I cheapening my attractiveness if someone sees me across different platforms? (Note: I've never recognized someone IRL from seeing them on an app before)

• Does scarcity in app-use translate to higher-value worth and status?

JOB APPLICATIONS:

• Do I play a likelier short-game and focus on finding roles I'm 100% qualified for?

• Do I cast a wide net towards even greater roles?

• Do I apply LinkedIn's girl scout-y badge of unemployment honor and risk appearing too needy? (Especially when all there is to say is that which I know to be true already: I. am. employable.)

• Why aren't there #DesperatetoWork or #ForcedtoWork badge levels?

For those out there trying, it's important that we consider these hard questions. Perhaps first among them: Do you tiptoe carefully down each decision, calculating prospective leads and draft replies, waiting with keen, long-game tactics? Or do you dive into the deep end with an awkward wedgie, creating waves from your signature jackknife style–it always achieves maximum displacement, er, value—which may or may not hit someone with just the right amount of force to pick you for their team?

The voice in my head tells me to be brave. Jump! This mindset worked when I made the best decision of my life thus far. Plus there's the fact that Travis Kelce's mom made a similar concession when endorsing her son's dating style: shoot for the stars.

If you're still reading, my goal is to share strategies. I'm not going to call them successful, or semi-so, as some are pending. My secondary goal is to make you laugh and feel a kinship in the struggle of finding what we want, or what we think we want, or at the very least – my personal priority – finding the starting blocks to something you can build upon, either in a company or human form.

I've organized my thoughts into 4 main stories (dare I say case studies?), each written with differing perspectives from dating and labor pools. They are:

1.) THE ONE WHERE THEY DON'T CALL YOU BACK
Dating:

You hit it off at a party. He's cute. Great smile. Your friend leaves the circle to give you space and as fate has it, he immediately turns and introduces himself, "I'm Garrett." He asks if you want a refill to which you say "YES" louder and faster than you meant to. He smiles and walks you to the kitchen where you exchange safe questions until glasses clink and he asks, "you on Insta?" You watch him type into the search bar on your phone. (His handle is FIRST NAME.LAST NAME -- a bit boring, but, hey, you are looking for stability.) The evening progresses on a couch, conversing with good eye contact (under 3 seconds not creepy type), and he even tells you he's a touchy feely kind of guy before asking to hold your hand and caress your knee cap. He's meeting up with friends so the night ends with next week inquiries. You accept his Insta request and follow back. Next week he's watching all your stories. He hearts them. By the following week he hasn't initiated anything though. You send a DM asking if he wants to grab a drink. He never replies. He continues to watch your stories. He still hearts them. You are confused. You send one more DM -- a casual, "u around this weekend?" — before giving up on seeing him again. A month later you accidentally click on his story reel and see him traveling with a girl. Oh well.

Job Search:

You manage to see a posting early enough that you're in the first ten applicants, according to LinkedIn. A week later you receive a voicemail from Sofia, the hiring manager, asking for a call back if you're still interested. You call back immediately. But it's been a few hours – *damn!* – and instead of connecting with Sofia, you leave her an unpracticed (though concise) voicemail with your name and number, confirming you are, in fact, definitely, very interested in learning more about the role. You hang up and worry you may have said the word "definitely" twice. Days go by. You find Sofia's email on LinkedIn and decide to send a friendly email confirming your (definite) interest and desire to connect. You notice she's viewed your profile in the past 4 days. You conclude she must have viewed your page before she called. A few more days go by before you decide to make one more effort -- a casual voicemail, ten seconds max, because she doesn't pick up again. Weeks go by. One day you notice the open job posting is no longer there. Wasn't meant to be.

2.) THE INCONSISTENT 'TEXTER'
Dating:

Your second and third date go surprisingly well. You've been trying to keep zero expectations of where things are going but it's hard because there's chemistry. He's not a great texter but he's Spanish, and your friend Ygnacio says that's normal. (He calls you, anyway, and that's proof of something). Last weekend you were hanging out IRL and he said, "let's do something next weekend." Which is now. No word from him, you don't reach out either, and end up spending the evening with your Italian friend Alessandro cooking gnocchi from scratch – not a wasted evening at all. You wake up to a text you missed (because you were having fun) where he asks, "You can do tomorrow?" You wait to reply, "drinks or din, both?" because it's early. He replies quickly, smiley emoji. You interpret this to mean IT'S ON. Around midday, the next day, you text to confirm details. No response. By the time you realize you should have just called it's 7pm, you decide to follow up with an easy text, "still down?" Maybe he's taking a disco nap. Maybe he's busy. (He's not one of those glued-to-the-phone types!) You are looking cute in a black dress and combat boots. You join up with friends at a club, in Malasaña – not a wasted evening at all. In the morning you see two texts from him. The first at 10pm: "We can do drinks & catchup?" and a second a little after 12am: "in Malasaña!" So close, and yet, quite far.

Job Search:

You make it to the fourth round of interviews. Apparently the last one. You're proud of yourself. You should be. You initially poached a connection off LinkedIn, a cold call, which led to a door opening. While you don't consider yourself a great salesperson, you keep authentic relationships across all areas of your life. You bring your whole self to work (your *professional* whole self, that is). The interview process this time around is enjoyable. You haven't had to try that hard. You think, *this company wants me for me.* After the first interview with the hiring manager, Jennifer, it took three weeks to hear back, but hear back you did. The second interview was similar. It required waiting two weeks, just to hear, "We are still in the interview process with other candidates." You've mastered the casual hello. They know you wish them well. Jennifer and you have rapport. And she informs you of a likely update next week. So, you email, casually, next Friday morning. No response for a week. You try calling. Still, no response. You're left with a puzzling thought. Is Jennifer OK? Did her appendix burst before she could put up an away message, or is this a classic story of rejection? Missed connections are so sad emoji.

3.) THE ONE THAT COULD BREAK YOUR HEART

Dating:

Somehow the Raya Gods have smiled down on you and the cute guy with humble-looking eyes and normal pics (read: no shirtless mirror selfies) messages first with a personal greeting which shows he's read your profile. You exchange pleasantries and cell numbers. More messages ensue. The next day he leaves a voice note that makes you laugh. Exchanges continue, which lead to phone calls, and then an intro facetime — you live in different cities. You can't imagine anything more awkward. But it goes just fine, and he looks the same (phew! you've been catfished before!). Actually, he is handsome-r than you expected. You agree to meet IRL because texting without meeting only leads to a strange reality where relationships don't really exist. Because you're not comfortable flying to meet someone—omg the pressure—you ask him to see you instead, and he does. He flies up, on a plane, had to buy a ticket, to see you.

In return for effort and doing what he said he was going to do (you're not used to that), you plan a great weekend. You squeeze multiple dates into two days. You get to know each other over dinners, drinks, walking, laughing, etc. He tells you he had a great time. You did too. And you think you may *like-like* him, so you're fearful of how things will progress. Uncertainty of what will happen now that planning a weekend is over sinks in, and while texts and chats continue, their pace enters an unknown trajectory of emotions.

Job Search:

A company you love, located in a city you love, with a salary you love, lists a job posting that accurately describes YOU and your amazing skillsets. You manage to find the ear of the HR manager through a family friend who always replies, "No problem!" and forwards your, "I just applied to [INSERT ALL THE COMPANY NAMES], do you know anyone open to a referral?" email for the one-hundred-and-seventy-fifth time. The HR manager endorses your CV and sets up a second interview with the SVP, whom you'd work closely under. Your interview goes great. You sell yourself. You, my dear, are *authentic*. You know this because she says, "I think you're terrific," and, "You seem very smart," and, "I like your energy"— I swear all of that — at the end, before she confides you're one of three candidates she's focused on (out of 100!). Updates to come next week. Everything seems right. You stop yourself from looking at apartments in the area because, well, you're suddenly superstitious. Is it wise to plan that far ahead, for something you don't have? At least you know you want it.

4.) THE ONE WHERE THEY FINALLY CALL YOU BACK (...BUT THEN GHOST YOU FR)

Dating:

You're leaving the country in 3 days. You open Instagram to an alert that Garrett has replied, finally, that is, if you can call it that as he doesn't address your last message. He comments on a picture of suitcases by asking, "You still single?" with the smiley side-eye emoji that's up to no good. It's cringe but you still think he's hot. Why not have an excuse to say goodbye to your favorite bar? You reply, "I am. But you have a GF?" You see him *typing...* immediately. He says, "Not anymore. Would love 2 c u. Tomorrow 8p?" You know this is going nowhere but you also love to make out. You confirm a thumbs up emoji because you're in your mid-30's and 'old people' use that one the most (supposedly mid-30's is old). Tomorrow comes and around 5pm you text, asking where to meet. You shave your legs and. are. ready. 7pm rolls around. Then 8:30pm. You decide to join your friends who have gathered at a terrace, you were planning to see them anyway. The evening goes with no further communication from Garrett. Zilch. Zero. You think maybe he's tripped and fallen into a ditch. Maybe he took a nap and forgot to set an alarm. Maybe. The truth? You will never see him again, and that's OK. You hope he gets better at talking to girls.

Job Search:

You're reviewing your cover letter for a corporate real estate job when *suddenly* CBRE emails to schedule The Final Interview. You've only been waiting four weeks with no update. (You didn't think it went well *and* she called you Christine instead of Christie). You suppose your well-articulated summations of accomplishments were soothing to their ears. You, after all, do sound confident when you talk because, you've done a lot of shit. The Final Interview is onsite! You're going to meet the team! You would be leading a subregion, five managers from six assets, all part of the same REIT. Oh, and your salary? 25% higher than the one you left before heading to graduate school. You can visualize the commute. But first, you wait to confirm the time. You've given the EA a broad range of hours, anytime next Monday to Friday. You wait a day to call. You wait two days to call again. Between email follow ups and another left-voicemail you decide to give up because it's their job to reply. If nothing ever comes of it, that's just the way it goes, you guess.

Christie Clark is currently writing her first book, *The Trick of Birth*. She claims to write for fun, and loves creative nonfiction and poetry. You can find her on Substack @CCMarieClark.

The Law of Return

By Shanti Ariker

The Regular Army
November 1987

"Look at that strange thing in the sky," I heard someone say as I exited the barracks. I had just placed my kitbag containing everything I possessed in the country on a thin mattress inside. I was dressed in my army Class *Bets* — the uniform you wear on base — a drab olive-green that matched the glints in my hazel eyes when the sun shone down. I was reacquainting myself with the feel of wearing my black boots again. My dirty-blonde hair fell right around shoulder-length. I looked up but didn't see anything unusual, so I wasn't nervous yet.

The sparse rocky, brown terrain landscape surrounded the base. Whatever plants were around from what I could see had turned yellow from lack of rain. I spied a border fence a few hundred meters behind the back of our base.

I heard a thump just then followed by gunshots. The wireless radio came to life with orders barked out clipped, staccato-like in Hebrew. I couldn't understand it all.

I asked the first soldier I saw, "What's going on?"

"Sounds like a terrorist attack," he said.

Now I was nervous.

I'd been in the Israel Defense Forces for a full year already, but I had only arrived three hours prior at what was to be my new base in Northern Israel, part of the artillery branch of the army. The base was in what is called 'the finger of the Galilee,' hugging the Lebanese border squeezed just north of *Kiryat Shmona*, itself only two kilometers south of the border. I didn't know a soul there, and here I was in the eye of the storm.

I saw an attractive blonde soldier with a buzz-cut, his three-striped shoulder insignia indicating he was a non-commissioned officer. He glanced at me curiously as he walked towards the medic's office, marked with a red Jewish star, standing for emergency medical services, called '*Magen David Adom*' in Hebrew. I didn't say anything, still trying to assess the situation. As I walked towards the base's center, I looked up to the sky again. This time, I saw the afternoon sun reflecting off a long, rectangular shape, just as the object began its descent into a nearby area beyond our base's perimeter.

Male soldiers dressed in olive-green uniforms and black boots matching mine ran towards jeeps parked in a row near the rear of the base. Other soldiers rushed to the armored personnel carriers I could see peeking behind the medic's barrack. Still more male soldiers sprinted by me — at least thirty of them — donning their helmets and grabbing long Israeli-made *Galil* machine guns. The soldiers slung their guns over their shoulders and swarmed the front gate like a marauding herd of wildebeests, yelling to the others to grab supplies and get in the nearby jeeps. Jeeps laden with equipment and men sped through the front gate and past the guard who stood sentinel there.

Udi, the second in command on the base, yelled for the female soldiers to gather in the women's barracks.

Six of us female soldiers were soon huddled together inside, a few sitting on folding chairs in the middle of the bunk beds, others on mattresses. I hadn't yet met any of them. I surveyed the room, attempting to suss out the leader of the group.

There was one man in the room. This rather petite guy looked to be of Moroccan or Yemenite descent, dark-skinned and with black, closely cropped hair. Not like the guys I had crushes on in my high school football team back in California; more like a theater kid or one of the nerds. He sat on a chair in the middle of the room. His knees were up against his chest, his black boots barely worn in, still shiny from the last polishing and resting on the seat of his chair. He had his head between his knees. When he looked up, I thought he might be sick any minute.

One of the girls whispered to me that he was the troop barber. He was the only one in the barracks with a gun, but I could see that he would not be any help to us if the female soldiers were in danger. That's probably why he had been spared running around where the real action was outside.

I felt sorry for him, but he also annoyed me. He was supposed to be a soldier. A warrior. Overcoming his fear to protect his country and fellow soldiers. But here he was, looking lost and scared. It wasn't making me feel confident or protected.

Would I have to take matters into my own hands? I was scared, too. The need for self-preservation had taught me that I would be ready to grab the gun. But would it help? The few times I had shot a gun I didn't have the best aim. Why were we huddled inside when all the action was outside? I knew that women weren't allowed to fight in combat, but I was at a combat outpost on the border so being put in a shelter to be guarded by a man who was more scared than me seemed wrong. But there was nothing I could do about it.

Bunk beds lined each wall, enough for eight female soldiers. Some of us sat on chairs in the middle of the room. One or two women were huddled together on a bed, sitting with their legs crossed or lying on their stomachs with their arms propping up their heads.

The air was electric, pulsating with energy all around us while we sat quietly, awaiting word inside our barrack. We couldn't see what was happening outside. By this time, most of the men had exited the base, leaving a small contingent behind to guard.

I had to steel myself for what might come. I wanted to look like I was ready for anything, even if I didn't feel like it. How was I supposed to be prepared for an attack?

I assessed the group again. Would I be able to fit in with these Israeli *sabras*? They were not like the immigrant group I had just left. That was good and bad all at once. *Sabra* was a fitting way to describe Israelis as I'd come to know them, a Hebrew moniker for the prickly pear fruit: tough on the outside but sweet on the inside.

The wireless radio was silent for the moment. A light-skinned woman with a pixie haircut was the first to speak, her voice shaking as she cried. "I want to go home. I don't understand why we need to stay here."

"Calm down," said a girl with brown hair and large, circular glasses with thick black frames, who I later learned was named Iris. She sat on a chair, one of her lanky legs in a figure four pose across the other one. I detected a very slight American accent and found out later that she had been born in the States. "It's not like we can just pick up and leave," Iris continued. "The terrorists are now to the south of us. We can't leave our base anytime we want anyhow. You know that."

The first girl sniffed and blew her nose. She was crying softly. I didn't feel much better, but there was no way I would cry. I was already a master of hiding how I felt, a skill I had honed most of my childhood.

There had been no major terror attacks in Israel since earlier that year. I would be lying if I said I had thought for one minute that an attack would happen to me. And certainly not on the first day I arrived back in the regular army. I hadn't really thought much about being placed in harm's way, since nothing remotely dangerous had happened to me since I arrived in the country.

What had I gotten myself into? I felt sick to my stomach thinking about it being in the middle of an attack. I could have stayed put on the *kibbutz*, the communal farm where I had been preparing fifth graders for their day. I could have completed my army service with my immigrant unit. Safe and sound behind the barbed wire that protected the *kibbutz* where we were living, situated near Jordan, a relatively safe border.

We had turned off the lights in the base to hide it from the terrorist that was still at large. We lit the entirety of the barracks with a small lamp. Nothing but each other and the wireless radio to keep us company. Occasionally, we heard a command relayed but we couldn't tell much about what was going on beyond the gates of our outpost.

Everyone stayed quiet, staring at nothing. Udi swung the door open, a cigarette tucked behind his ear. Udi had driven me up to the base after my lunch at the armored Northern Command base.

Shanti Ariker is a lawyer writing her memoir about surviving a childhood of well-publicized, ideologically-driven custody battles by finding strength as a soldier in the Israeli army. Find more about her at ShantiAriker.com.

Jack London and Me
by Linda Ballou

Trotting behind my guide along the trails that Jack London once rode, I imagined myself as one of the many friends he led on horseback rides through his 1,400 acre Beauty Ranch in the early 1900's. We galloped through stands of Eucalyptus, Madrano, and towering Redwood trees shading the fern-filled glens that were just as Jack described them in his novel *The Valley of the Moon*. Delighted with each new vista, I too felt "vitalized, organic" as I overlooked the wine vineyards in neat, tidy rows stretching to the foot of the purple Sonoma Mountains. We cantered over a rise to see the lake that Jack and Charmian, his wife of eleven years, swam in on sunny afternoons. I saw myself gliding with them through the clear water; drying on a hot rock in the sun, cooled by the wisp of a breeze.

Like young Jack London, I went from California to the Northwest while in my teens. Unlike Jack, it was not my idea of a great adventure. My parents, determined to homestead in Haines, Alaska, rudely uprooted me and took me to a world populated by loggers, fishermen, and Tlingit Indians. At thirteen, I hadn't read Jack's *White Fang* or *The Call of the Wild*. I didn't know I was walking in the famous author's footsteps when I took the narrow gauge train that snakes up the Whitehorse Pass into the Yukon. I had no idea it was the alternate route for the Chilkoot Trail Jack climbed, carrying a 150-pound pack, during the Gold Rush of the 1890s.

A decade after my family's shift to the north, Hollywood chose to use the more accessible Dalton Trail from Haines to the Klondike to re-enact the fabled climb of the stampeders up the ice steps of the Chilkoot Trail in the movie *White Fang*. Every able-bodied person in my hometown was hired to re-create the famous scene Jack described. Even then, while everyone in town swaggered about bragging about his, or her role in the film, I still had no personal awareness of Jack London. He was simply an adventurer who captured the grit of the northwest in "children's books."

It was not until my own personal call to adventure, took me to Hawai'i, that I tasted the vitality of Jack's writing. I found solace in the gentle beauty of the Islands, and envied the athletic bodies of the Hawaiians and their connection with the sea and nature. While living on Kauai, I came to respect and admire their culture and began to delve into the history of old Hawaii. It was here that the seed for my historical novel, *Wai-nani: A Voice from Old Hawai'i*, took root. In my research, I was pleasantly surprised to find Jack London's Hawaiian stories.

Jack London made the "blue-water crossing" to the Territory of Hawaii in 1907 from San Francisco on the barely sea-worthy Snark. "The Sailor on Horseback" sailed for two years throughout the South Seas collecting adventures for his stories. Over a period of thirteen years he returned many times to Hawai'i, his favorite resting spot. He showed great aloha (love) for the Islands and loved to hear the stories of the Kanaka and delved deep into the myths of old Hawaii handed down in the chants of elders. While writing my fictionalized account of the life of Ka'ahumanu, the favorite wife of

Kamehameha the Great, I read Jack's Hawai'i stories for inspiration and insight into the minds of the ancients. I studied the techniques used by the master of engaging writing and prayed that what I absorbed would filter through my own writing.

After roaming the globe Jack came home to his Beauty Ranch where he died at forty from uremic poisoning. After my ride, I sought out his simple gravesite surrounded by a weathered wooden fence. By this time I had read all of Jack's major works and a couple of books written about him. I felt a spiritual connection with a man who died a century ago. It seemed he had been with me all my life, forging ahead of me, sharing his insights, giving me guidance from the grave. For me there was no time between us. The man who religiously wrote a thousand words a day departed in silence. No one spoke at his service, as though there were no more words left to say.

Years after my visit to Beauty Ranch, I found the memory of Jack London again at the Huntington Hartford Museum in Pasadena. I was drawn to a collection of letters written in his hand. "Writing is about action, struggle, conflict and resolution," he said. Jack spent many hours reading the work of novices, editing their pieces and giving words of encouragement. Tears streamed uncontrollably as turbulent emotions rose from deep inside. Writing, often a thankless, unnoticed endeavor, had great urgency for me once more. I wanted to thank Jack London for his kindness and generosity of spirit. Though I don't possess the fire to blast through life like a fleeting meteor shower as Jack London did, I do strive to write consistently. I try not to be afraid to write about what is important to me and to be honest with my readers. I look to him for strength on those days when my soul cries tired.

Linda Ballou has been writing for her life from her isolated teen years in Southwest Alaska to her reflective years in an artistic enclave in Los Angeles. Two historical novels inspired by defiant females and one new adult novel with a feisty female protagonist are the result of her efforts. Along the way she sought out the most beautiful locations on the planet and wrote three travel books extolling the transformative effects of nature on the receptive soul. Learn more about her work at LindaBallouAuthor.com

Lights, Camera, Consent: How Women in Film Are Changing Our Minds About Sex

by Sharon Beck-Doran

In August of 2023, a monumental thing happened: *Barbie* the movie broke $1B at the global box office. Only 53 films in history have been able to do that, and this was the first directed by a woman. If you're like me, the importance of this didn't sink in right away. *What is the big deal?* I wondered.

What I didn't know is that in the short history of film, the stories told have been almost exclusively from the male perspective. Of the 53 films to hit $1B, only 9 center around a female protagonist, assuming you count the fish *Dory* and three Disney Princesses. Since 1929 when the Oscars began, only 3 women have won best director and only 7 have been nominated. Of the 581 movies nominated for best picture only 18 were directed by women.

Why is this significant? Why is it important that our entertainment, our imaginary escape from the real world, tell women's stories?

Something clicked when I listened to actor-director Rachel Bloom talk about the recent push in Hollywood to include women as directors and in the writers room. Bloom is best known as the star, co-creator, writer and executive producer of the hit TV show *Crazy Ex-Girlfriend.*

Bloom explained that sex scenes are changing. That pattern where the guy grabs the girl, kisses her and they fall into bed together, no words needed—that's actually very similar to porn, she said. *Damn,* I thought, *mind blown.* I had never made that connection.

The conversation reminded me of one of the few times I saw a love scene that depicted a man putting on a condom. By depicted, I mean you saw their silhouettes and it took a minute to guess what he was doing. The movie was *Love & Basketball* (2000) written and directed by Gina Prince-Bythewood. The scene left me feeling vicariously loved and cared for.

The storyline of Love & Basketball follows Quincy and Monica who have been playing basketball together since they were kids. They eventually fall in love. Both aspire to careers as pro basketball players, but Monica is the more talented of the two. Conflict arises over who's success would come first and who would sacrifice for the other's career. The closing scene shows Monica playing for the WNBA as Quincy holds their little girl, cheering her on from the sidelines.

Seeing Quincy relinquish his dream to find a new identity as a father and husband is compelling. I expect I wasn't the only woman who left the theater thinking *Damn! I want a man like that!—One that isn't intimidated by my success.*

Could a man tell the same story? Of course, but would he?

As a guest on Dax Shepherd's podcast, *Arm Chair Expert*, Salma Hayek told the story of her first sex scene in the 1995 movie *Desperado* with Antonio Banderas. The scene was not in the original script, but studio executives demanded it after they saw the chemistry between Banderas and Hayek.

Hayek knew the movie was a big break in her career so she couldn't say, "No." She recounted the experience saying she was terrified and cried the entire time. They cleared the room, attempting to make her feel more comfortable. The director pieced together clips between sobs to make it work. The question of her consent wasn't even a question.

In 2017 stories began to emerge of Hollywood executive Harvey Weinstein manipulating young women into giving sexual favors for the promise of career opportunities. In response, women began to courageously share their stories of workplace abuse with the hashtag #metoo. It started a movement.

Consent in the entertainment industry became a major topic of conversation. These women's stories exposed an entertainment industry that had nurtured a culture of sexual abuse.

Actors and production companies have started to require Intimacy Coordinators. The purpose of this new role is to ensure that actors consent to everything that happens while filming sex scenes.

It doesn't sound sexy to have carefully coordinated and mutually agreed upon rules established well before anyone takes off their clothes, but planning is valuable. Sometimes people need a little time to consider what they are comfortable doing or showing. When a person is asked in front of cast and crew they might say "yes" to things they wouldn't want to do if they had less pressure and a few minutes to think about it. Instead of a culture of abuse, the film industry is working to develop a culture of safety and consent.

Most of us don't go to the movie theater, read a novel or turn on the TV to engage in existential reflection. We want to be entertained. We look to escape the reality of our everyday lives and get caught up in stories that make us feel something—excited, in love, aroused, moved or inspired.

Whether we like it, hate it, or even refuse to recognize it, movies and TV shape the way we see the world. That's especially true for sex. In that very intimate place, books, movies, TV and porn are often the only thing we know of sex outside our own experiences.

Our lived experiences as men and women not only affect the stories we tell, but also the way that we tell them. Slowly, the influence of women in entertainment is changing the conversations we have about sex. Our view of what good looks like is starting to include phrases like, "Would you like me to stop?" We need more of this. Film and TV can help women understand their own stories and set new expectations for sexual consent.

Sharon Beck-Doran is a recovering evangelical and writes about faith and sexuality from her home in Kansas City, KS. You can find more of her work at RelevantFaithJourney.com

Like Mother

by Elisa L. Bozmarova

Dear *Mamo*,

I'm replying to your letter. It's the only one I've ever known you to write—the one you left on the desk in the hotel room on the 43rd floor. Sometimes I imagine that, during the night or the next morning, a cold wind blew into the open window, from the Pacific Ocean, across the Golden Gate Bridge's open arms, and fluttered the pages, or scattered them on the floor. The room was empty. At least that's how I heard it told.

You'd used four pages, both sides. Written in ballpoint pen, a letter to us—your family. Your children and husband. It was in cursive Bulgarian, so I've struggled over the years to piece together the meaning your handwriting carries, and the meaning of your signature on the bottom. A letter meant to be read not by us first, but by whoever entered your room next. Read first by whoever found you.

You wrote that you loved us very much. You wrote the word "very" twenty-one times before you took your life.

Almost two decades later, my time has come to burrow into your life, our relationship, and our family's secrets. Am I destined to turn out like you? I ask as I approach twenty-nine years old—the same age you were when you died.

Chapter 1: THE PHONE CALL

Walnut Creek, California, 2001

The phone rang. Its ring pierced the late afternoon silence in our apartment. I watched my father, whom I called *Tati*, pick it up, his back toward me. He stood in the hallway next to the kitchen. We were in Northern California, where you'd moved first on your own, in those months when we were separated because you and Tati needed space. This reunion in California was our last chance at a fresh start. We all knew it.

By this point, you'd been gone nearly twenty-four hours. You had wanted to be somewhere else. You'd said you wanted to spend the night with friends. Tati had pleaded with you to stay. This wasn't the first time you'd left. You'd been gone before, for a night or several days, without warning or explanation. He'd sit by the phone, calling and calling you. Instinctively I knew not to talk about these instances with friends at school—the days and nights when you would temporarily stop being a mother, removing the title like you'd take off an apron. I felt weird enough in my own skin—brown, with a funny name, always new in town, already about to move again.

Your leaving the house was always bad news. You and Tati always fought when you returned. But this time felt different. We still hadn't heard from you. Sunset felt heavy and final, a door locking shut. The Twin Towers had fallen eleven days before, along with those tiny people falling from the buildings—or had they jumped? I didn't know until years later that in those eleven days, you had openly spoken about those people and their choice to die that way. And even before then, in car rides near the

Golden Gate Bridge, you would point at the bridge's sweep of red metal and comment on the fact that many people jumped there, too.

A few weeks before the phone rang, we were all in the car. I sat behind you, invisible. I could see your curly hair peeking above your seat. Michael and Gabby sat to my left. Tati drove, his forearms tense at the wheel. You two were arguing as we approached a red light downtown. Then, you opened the car door. You stepped out of the car, shut the door, and walked away, leaving us behind at the light. We stared at you, watching you walk amid traffic with a calm and sense of purpose bordering on insane, praying that you would not get hit by a car.

So when Tati picked up the phone, I knew it was either you calling or someone else calling to give us news about you. I imagined you getting hit by a car. I imagined you lying in a hospital bed. I imagined we would have to visit you or pick you up or Tati would go, sighing, while I watched Michael and Gabby. My tenth birthday was ten days away. I was excited to hit double digits and that we were going to go to Six Flags.

I heard Tati telling the person on the phone that *no, that was no longer our address.* He sounded impatient, then panicked. He needed the person, who must have announced who they were, to tell him immediately why they were calling. *We've left Tulsa, yes. We are now in northern California. Originally from Bulgaria.*

We'd traveled through thirty U.S. states by the time I was nine. Tati, who knew better English, enrolled me in a different elementary school every few months to a year—seven schools by the time I was in fourth grade. I was proud of my ability to adapt, or to convince myself that adapting was good. Every cross-country move we made was predicated by the idea that things would change with the environment, that we needed a fresh start. And we got it: our Bulgarian culture faded. We faded. I was afraid of you for as long as I can remember. Now, in the decades that have passed since that afternoon when the phone rang, I say this without accusation or blame. You often created the circumstances from which we ran, or they were created around you, but it wasn't just you. We moved because something was missing. Nothing quite measured up to our American dreams.

Life was one long road trip: we threw away what we couldn't take in the car or in a U-Haul, sat shoulder-to-shoulder, and zigzagged across the country. We moved from the Eastern Bloc to California to Pennsylvania, then back to California, then Florida, then a journey through the Spanish moss-draped South to Oklahoma, and finally to northern California, where you and Tati decided to give your relationship one more chance.

Then the person on the other end said something I couldn't hear. Tati responded, "No," but it wasn't the answer to a question. He collapsed. Convulsing with sobs, he stumbled toward the living room. I ran from my room and climbed onto the couch with him to comfort him. Maybe you wouldn't know this—I had played this role before whenever you left. Michael and Gabby were still in our room, playing with my new kitten, a tabby named Hercules. You'd given him to me as an early birthday gift. I'd wondered why you had gotten it for me over a week before my birthday.

Outside the sky was cold blue, the coldest blue I'd ever seen it, as dusk shifted to night.

I asked him what happened.

"Mommy is dead," he said.

The human mind switches to shock when something happens that is simply beyond what it can comprehend, when the emotional stakes are off the scale. But this scale wasn't so foreign to me. You had tried to take your life before. Immediately, when he said those words to me, I felt what it was to lose you forever. The chasm you left swallowed me whole in its pitch-blackness. I am still writing myself out.

I asked Tati what happened to you. An instinctual part of me knew that this window of opportunity, before he became my father again and thought clearly about how to handle your passing, would soon close. I wanted the truth.

Someone had found your body that morning, before the door to your room was opened and they found your letter. The coroner's office in San Francisco thought we still lived in Oklahoma. They had been trying to reach us all day.

Michael and Gabby came out of the room. Tati took us out to the balcony. He got on his knees. Maybe in some liminal space after death when you can still see us, you found us there, on the balcony. The first thing he did after you died was he prayed. I still remember the prayer. He told God he knew that it wasn't God's fault, and prayed that God would forgive you. He prayed that God would protect us and tell him what to do next. The preacher he used to be returned for a moment from the dim past.

When we walked back into the living room, Tati called the police. I think he needed support and this seemed like the sturdiest kind. Two officers came to our house. I kept quiet. They explained to my brother and sister, at Tati's request, that our mother had died. Michael, a little older than our youngest sibling, began to cry. Gabby, only four years old, stood blank-faced. She did not seem to understand, and how could she? She hadn't had time to imagine her mother in the future. We had not just lost our mother that day, we had lost her every day to come.

Ellie Bozmarova (she/her) is a Bulgarian-American writer whose work has appeared in The Common, phoebe, Business Insider, and elsewhere. She holds an MFA in Creative Nonfiction from Goucher College and BA in English from UC Berkeley. Ellie is at work on a literary coming-of-age novel set in Bulgaria.

Always Go
by Girish Gupta

I didn't often make this sort of mistake. I was backed into a corner; the walls to my left and behind me funneled rocks, glass bottles and whatever other shrapnel protesters hurled right at me. They weren't aiming for me, rather for the Venezuelan soldiers lined up to my right. My camera lens was trained on the soldiers' weapons, ready for the next muzzle flash, though my eyes kept darting to the protesters lest they launch something more dangerous my way. Rocks and bottles smacked my helmet, as tear gas seeped into my mask.

I'd been in this type of environment countless times and was normally adept at positioning, getting a clear view, and taking down quotes, photos, and video, without putting myself in significant danger. I'd done this—as well as numerous hostile environment and self-defense courses—frequently enough to know that the best defense was thinking ahead: Make sure you have a way out and make sure you take it before things escalate. That is, don't get to where I was now.

Thankfully, I was well protected. Solid boots, shin pads, knee pads, a heavy-duty flak jacket, gas mask, and Kevlar helmet kept whatever landed from bothering me too much. The real dangers were flaming Molotov cocktails or live fire. Thankfully neither appeared in anyone's arsenal just yet.

Jhon, a young *Reuters* motorcyclist and regular partner on these outings, had made a run for it along the gap between protesters and soldiers. His hands eagerly beckoned me over. My calculation, however, was that following him was more dangerous than staying put. I'd rather crouch and wait it out with a few light smacks to my protective gear than be struck by something carrying far more momentum.

So I calmly waited, depressing my camera's shutter while looking around to ensure the scene didn't devolve.

But what was I doing here? There was barely a story to tell. News is deviation from the mean, and Venezuela's mean had descended in recent years precisely to what I was witnessing. The country was undergoing a humanitarian crisis, with millions earning a dollar a month, suffering food shortages, insecurity, and rampant inflation. I don't know how many times I wrote that sentence. Our headline at *Reuters* that day—April 4, 2017—was evergreen: "Venezuela security forces battle anti-Maduro protesters."

Here, on the ground covering one of the world's worst crises, was precisely the position I'd spent the last decade narrowly aiming for. And I'd made it, and made it with the world's top news outlet in a well-paid staff position. But what was my purpose?

Everybody around me was suffering, earning nothing, not eating properly, mentally distraught, seeding trauma that would last generations. I was to tell their story but doing so I'd learned, didn't make any difference. Was I actually just here for my own gratification—an adrenaline boost with which I could one day open a memoir?

I had wanted to impact the world, whatever that meant, but I could have done that in a more sophisticated way. And I'd chosen Venezuela on a whim. The foreign correspondent's destination, I'd later realize, is often a playground for the ego.

My mind wandered. I held no anger or resentment to either protesters or authorities—nor to those Venezuelan soldiers who had detained me a year earlier, nor to Egyptian military intelligence who had detained me four years earlier at the Suez Canal. I was good at being an impartial observer, not taking sides or becoming emotionally invested; that made me a better reporter. What angered me was the industry for which I was doing this—to which I was certainly not an impartial observer. I was tired of rampant mismanagement, exaggeration, and fabrication by the industry's most respected news outlets, and wild egos which trumped everything. I'd just returned from a disastrous trip to Iraq, in what had meant to be my next move. I'd felt betrayed too often, and here I was, being smacked around on a street corner while the editors from whom I sought support sipped cocktails at New York award ceremonies—and my family back home wondered what I was doing with my life.

After some twenty minutes, I managed to reunite with Jhon behind the soldiers as they pushed forward, and we rode his bike through side streets to join the protesters. I got my photos, quotes, and recorded a piece-to-camera before spending a relaxed evening with my girlfriend in our offensively cheap four-story penthouse. We watched macaws fly over Caracas as the sun set behind the Ávila mountain.

It was beautiful and thrilling. But something wasn't right.

Girish Gupta is a former foreign correspondent and photographer who spent nearly a decade reporting from Venezuela during the worst of its humanitarian crisis. His work has appeared everywhere from the *New Yorker* and *New York Times* to *TIME* and *Reuters*, where he was a Senior Correspondent. Gupta has also reported across the Americas, Middle East, and Asia. Raised by a tenacious immigrant mother, his pursuit of justice led him to journalism—though he became disillusioned by the industry he wanted to love.

The Last Father's Day

by Alissa Larson

My dad never got ties for Father's Day. He rarely wore them. He was a fishing lure man, a work gloves man, a good pair of socks and some chocolate covered cherries man.

My favorite, he was a cloth handkerchief man. An old-fashioned gentleman, he always carried two in his pocket, one for himself and one for a lady. It was usually reserved for my mom and his daughters. It would come out when a horse bucked us off, or when we fell off our bikes and scraped our knees, or when one of us had a cold and sat sniffling through church.

For his last Father's Day, my gift was a goodbye letter to him. I wrote about how I loved him, how he changed me, made me fierce and independent, good with tools, kind and generous, able to raise a daughter without a man because of the strength he gave me.

I watched as a horrified look crossed his eyes. He didn't accept my gift. He closed his eyes and passed it to my mother, saying, "I'm tired now."

The doctors had just told him his cancer was terminal. Something my sisters and I had understood for months seeing our broad-shouldered father starve and lose strength, always crippled with pain.

His blue eyes still sparkled with life, and he still had so many plans and dreams: to teach his grandson how to shoot a bow and arrow; to visit my house in California and ride horses with me in Yosemite; and most of all, to go on one last fishing trip with his girls.

That fishing trip was the gift I had tried to give him. I called every place in the tri-state area that might sell live fish. Sometimes I was begging and sobbing on the phone as Father's Day got closer. My plan was to put them in a shallow backyard kiddy pool and fish with him steps from his bed one last time. The last place I called said they would break the law and sell me live fish, but the man on the phone gently told me that they wouldn't survive in a backyard pool, even for a few moments.

With no fish, I tried to give him my letter instead, but he was not one for goodbyes. He didn't accept death and fought to live as long as humanly possible. There was nothing graceful about the way he left a few months later, he suffered and battled to the end.

At his funeral, I sat in the front row. Just me and my six sisters and mother. He couldn't pass us a cloth handkerchief that day for all of our tears. It felt like an insult when the pastor referred to him as a "man's man." "Look at all the strong women he left," I thought. We grew up to become firefighters and soldiers, artists, writers, teachers, and healers. He told us we could be anything and loved us, uniquely, individually. My eyes filled with tears over the injustice of his eulogy. But I realized no words would ever be a fitting tribute for him, or a fitting love letter from me. I think the birds are the only ones who could have done it.

I remember a particularly painful day for him, as he was gasping a bit for air. He came out to the living room, and we opened all the windows. It was a sunny summer day, and a breeze blew through the house. Mid-conversation he stopped us. "Wait, listen to the birds. Have you ever heard anything so beautiful?" He said it with awe and his bright eyes shone, like someone who had never heard birds sing before. Magically the simple bird songs transformed into the most beautiful sound in the world. Another gift to us.

I realized then he didn't want to say goodbye because he found so much beauty in life. Beauty in the simple, beauty in the struggle, beauty in the love, beauty in the never-ending possibilities. There was no way we could have accomplished all his last wishes because he would have just dreamed more dreams and found more unearthly bird songs to really and truly hear.

Alissa Larson is a retired firefighter living in the San Francisco Bay Area. She writes poetry and is working on a memoir that explores social justice issues for female firefighters. Find more of her work at AlissaLarson.com.

Polk Street Hustler 1979

by Rob Peters

Rain washed the streets of San Francisco, making the stench of desperation a little more tolerable.

A Datsun pulled into Frank Norris Alley and its driver waved me over.

Another pervert? Another married man? Another lonely old guy?

"Hi, how you doing? Looking for a date?" he asks softly.

"Depends on what you're looking for," I tell him. He looks harmless, but most of them do.

"Would you like to go for a ride?"

"Sure" I say, getting into the car. He's grey haired, chubby, belly against the steering wheel.

"My wife and kids are out of town. I've got the place to myself. We can go there," he reveals without hesitation.

Married men always seem to admit something before the dirty deed, I think to myself.

Not knowing much of the city and only aware of how to get to Polk Street from the Greyhound bus depot on Seventh between Market and Mission, I try to memorize the route as familiar territory disappears.

He smiles as we enter the freeway onramp, leaving downtown.

"How far do you live?" I ask nervously.

"Not too far."

About twenty minutes pass before we pull into the driveway of a small house, in what I would later learn is Daly City.

"We're here," he says, as I breathe a sigh of relief.

Framed family photos adorn a hallway wall. He leads me to a bedroom where a photo of a woman sits on a nightstand beside the bed.

"Is that your wife?" I ask.

"Yes," he replies. His voice (and demeanor) now sinister, tossing me pink panties from a dresser drawer. "Put this on."

By my eighteenth birthday, I was standing on street corners and in alleyways, picking up strange men for whatever amount of cash they were willing to spend. Hustling had risks, but always a steady trade, and for an unemployable teenager without skills sometimes the only option.

During the late 1970s through early 1980s, gayborhoods distinguished the city's various LGBTQ subcultures: men with mustaches and tight 501's were known as Castro Clones, leather types and sadomasochists existed South of Market Street (on and around Folsom), trans the Tenderloin, while minorities and underage youth (mostly runaways) congregated in Polk Gulch.

Not all the boys engaged in sex work for survival, with many migrating from small towns, simply seeking out a gay life. Being minors it was a gayborhood where one could frequent bars such as Polk Gulch Saloon or Q.T. (the latter, a notorious hustler bar), and occasionally meet a sugar daddy.

Sometimes we'd put our earnings together for a place to stay for a night, shower and sleep, safe from the streets. A few of my buddies would seek quarters for the laundromat, from an organization that would later become Larkin Street Youth Services.

A lot of hustlers would utilize Leland Hotel, across the street from Q.T., which also had an adjacent alley for discreet pickups. Polk Street and Frank Norris Alley became a competitive and coveted corner. Ironic, considering an elementary school bordered the alley, with innocent children playing during recess, and not-so-innocent boys loitering day (and night) only steps away.

The police turned a blind-eye to activities on Polk, yet boys would always look out for Mary (street slang for law enforcement). Once, I was questioned by two officers and lectured about cruising, but that was it. They didn't care.

Never asking my age, for ID, or where I lived. Whenever there were police or vice officers patrolling Polk, we'd walk ahead of them alerting others, "Here comes Mary."

In the recently published *Kids on the Street*, author and historian Joseph Plaster quotes a 1984 news report, exposing "40 to 50 hardcore juvenile prostitutes are on that street at any one time." The following year, a newspaper story revealed further, "On a typical night, teenage boys can be seen loitering in doorways, offering their bodies for hire."

Like many runaway, homeless boys and men, my friend Richard and I hustled while simultaneously exploring our sexuality.

Richard and I had hitched a ride to San Francisco with a guy we'd met in Sacramento. Limited in funds, and not yet familiar with the city, the man promised he'd drop us off where we needed to be.

"Hi, how are you?" the radical faerie asked as I entered Miz Brown's corner café at Polk and Pine Streets.

"Good," I answered, taken aback by the stranger's appearance. A man with a mustache, wearing sandals, tattered jeans, a frilly blouse, and straw hat with flowers.

"Do you know how to apply lipstick?" he asked.

"No."

"Well then, sit down, and let me teach you."

It was my earliest encounter on Polk, while waiting for Richard to return from turning his first trick. Not always a harmless adventure, I spent many hours huddled in cold doorways with my street family, which included fourteen-year-old Joey and sixteen-year-old Geneva.

I developed street smarts while hustling, my first lesson from Joey: boys didn't have pimps, we were independent. He warned me of the dangers no boy should ever know. The day before we met, he'd jumped out of a second-story window to escape violence.

The streets were not kind to Joey, and I witnessed his decline. By the time he reached sixteen, he became drugged-out, used, abused, and discarded by sadists in the dungeons around Folsom Street.

My exposure to the South of Market S&M scene would unfortunately involve becoming handcuffed, gagged, and used after being misled by a trick who picked me up on Polk. He was a well-respected executive chef at both an upscale department store in Union Square and private club, who had a secret desire to torture.

"Hi, would you like to go for a ride, to my place on Potrero Hill?"

He drove a luxury car, so I figured why not? On the way to his home, I envisioned he might be a sugar daddy.

"Here, put these on," he whispered, tossing me handcuffs.

"Why? What are you going to do?"

"Don't worry. I won't hurt you. Just relax," he assured me, before offering a drink.

With cuffs on, next came a pair of socks. One stuffed in my mouth, the other tied around my head to hold it in place.

I went numb, for hours, unable to escape or yell for help.

Incapacitated, I stared out the window at San Francisco Bay while enduring his cruelty, eventually passing out.

When I woke from the assault he nonchalantly said, "I'm sorry. I didn't mean for it to go that far."

Us forgotten boys kept each other abreast of these violent tricks, which happened more often than we were willing to admit. But we kept each other company until a stranger took one of us away, and later looked to make sure the other had made it back safely.

My buddies on the street were misfits left to survive by whatever means necessary.

Geneva became the first hustler I'd met to contract the emerging AIDS virus. Homeless and without access to medical care, he stood no chance against the disease.

My nights on Polk Street would eventually come to an end. I was no longer a teenager and couldn't compete with fourteen or sixteen-year-olds, not even eighteen-year-olds.

I began venturing into the rougher Tenderloin district, specifically to Campus All-Male Theatre. Its ad touted, "Home of the Varsity Strip Squad and featuring the hottest and horniest performers on the West Coast. Live on stage and in the audience, all nude, all hard for you."

Straight (or bi) guys, otherwise known as "trade," could be found at the triple-x theatre and strip club. Not surprising to see a girl drop off her boyfriend, and an hour later he'd be onstage totally nude, while dozens of men fondled the stripper's derriere. Dates for later were also arranged.

How could I not explore my sexuality at a time when San Francisco was the center of the universe for lesbian, gay, bisexual, and transgender?

I was a boy who became a man during the golden age of gay life, and miraculously survived the AIDS pandemic at a time of great experimentation in my personal life.

Realizing no teenage boy should ever have to sell himself to survive became my catalyst from shame. For too long I held guilt that I was a terrible person because I hustled.

Reflecting on that time in my life, I now realize how dangerous it was for me to be where I was and how lucky I am to still be alive.

Rob Peters began a cathartic and transformative journey through the truth of memoir. Empowered by the sexual abuse survivor #MeToo social justice movement, combined with concern over reemergence of racial hatred and homophobia in America, his writing reflects both its history and consequence. This inspiring story of survival begins with coming of age and coming out in 1970s California. Read more about Rob and his forthcoming memoir via SidewalkIndian.com.

Chief Intuitive Officer:
The Secret Guide to Unlocking the Chakras of Success

by Alexandra Phillips

Back in the 80s when I was a free-range unsupervised kid growing up in NYC, one of my favorite things to do was to walk down Broadway to Barnes and Noble. I think it's important to note here how cool Barnes and Noble used to be. It was not fancy; it did not have a coffee shop in it. It was cool. But I digress.

At 11-years old I would tuck away in the occult section sitting on the floor, reading for hours. There I had a tendency to make friends with the people the city had forgotten. Judith—a 40-year-old divorcee used to find me in my corner of the bookstore and ask for palm readings. The newsstand guy who couldn't look anyone in the eye, would ask me for news from his recently deceased mom. And the owners of *Yees Laundry* on 93rd street would count on me to tell them what the weather would be days in advance because I had a 'magical face.'

Quickly I had a significant library of my favorites about astrology, palmistry, clairvoyance, and lucid dreaming. I would read these books until they were tattered and water-stained; keeping a stack in the bathroom to read in the one room of our NYC apartment where you could lock a door.

By the time I was in high school I was desperate for a tarot deck. I had my heart set on a Witch deck, and I would go visit it at the bookstore near my high school in Brooklyn almost daily. It was all I wanted, and when my friends and I did a holiday exchange I was sure I would get it. They got me the Rider Waite deck and while I was touched by the gift, I was also curious as to why they didn't get the Witch one. "We don't want you to be too weird," my friend Sarah said. "You're already too witchy," she said with a genuine smile.

What was so dangerous about being "too witchy?" I knew I was different. I knew ahead of time, when we were about to run into someone on the street, even though they lived on the other side of the city. I knew stories about people before they told me, and yes, I could also see and talk to ghosts. I assumed these were good things, special gifts that everyone would want. Wouldn't I want to be *more* witchy? Why did I need to keep these things secret? But often I was chastened to 'keep it to myself.'

"Don't talk so much, Alex, you upset people."

"You shouldn't know what you know."

This is the witch wound. The silencing of our intuitive gifts. This was not the first time I was told that I would be considered "too much," and it certainly wouldn't be the last. But it sticks with me because it was one of the first times I was asked to silence what I knew I should champion. My friends were just trying to protect me. Or possibly themselves. Because, what happens when we share our gifts? Well, History tells us that is when people start gathering the kindling. What is more dangerous than a powerful woman who calls her power back to herself? Nothing.

A woman who acknowledges and leans on her intuition to guide her is beyond dangerous, because she is not *in need.* Think of every time you were not attached to the outcome of something. Maybe it was a presentation, or a proposal, or even a romantic interest. If you don't need any particular outcome, it goes your way, 100% of the time.

I once led a workshop for women executives on how to hone their negotiation skills. This was for a very well-known company, and I was asked to take the word 'intuition' out of my workshop description. I was told it was too 'girly'. I'll get on my soapbox about the preposterous absurdity of taking intuition away from women leaders when they are negotiating another time; but I'll tell you when I was asked, I obliged. I wanted the gig. Again, I was being asked to silence my power. I was again, *Too Much.*

I have had a hard time writing this book. Here I am again, faced with the incongruity of me. I am not all witch. I am an executive. I am a powerful business owner and advisor. I can tell you how to trim a P&L for a higher return, or how to get acquisition-ready. And I can also tell you before you tell me with words, about what happened to you when you were nine that you haven't told anyone since. I can often channel or speak with energy that has passed to the spirit side. And I'm not going to lie to you, sharing my gifts is scary. So scary in fact, that about 20-years ago I took them all and put them in a metaphorical box and dug a pit so deep I was sure they would never see the light of day again. I spent a lot of time 'business-ing.' I spent so much time proving that I could walk the walk and talk the talk of business that I almost forgot who I was. But when you plant magic beans you better be ready for the beanstalk to grow, whether you want it to or not.

One day when I was walking down Van Brunt in Brooklyn I looked up and saw a crow. Without meaning to, I had an entire conversation with her. I laughed at myself, thinking I was silly for thinking that the crow and I were really talking. The next day when I went out to the car, there was not one, but 15 crows sitting on my car. No other car had a single bird near it. But after that it was like the floodgates opened. It was as though 20-years of beanstalks shot up at once. And it's been a rather wild ride since.

Sometimes, I do worry what others will think of me when they know what I can do, but I also wanted you to know that you can too. Your intuition is a muscle that can be strengthened. You just need to exercise it. Some people can naturally play basketball, others take to the piano with all their lifetimes of music literally at their fingertips. Some show up on this planet and can easily move between different languages. I showed up being able to speak energy.

This book is for all the intuitive leaders out there to help you hone your intuitive gifts. This is for witches who are business leaders and leaders who are witch-curious. I am tired of feeling like I have to prove myself to be part of any club. So, I am making my own club for intuitive leadership, and you are invited. The only criterion for this club is that anyone who wants to join can. The rules for membership are kindness, curiosity, and courage—however that makes sense for you. Only white light magic is welcome in this circle.

This is a choose your own adventure story. You can stick with the business examples at the start of each chapter. We can take the temperature of the water together by connecting the Root Chakra to the leadership capacity of Trust, and how that is the base of the pyramid for any successful team or business. I will share real world examples of how building the capacity of Trust has a measurable ROI. And not just in soft skills but on your bottom line. Or you can jump into the deep end and go all out witch with me at the end of each chapter with rituals that strengthen and align your Root Chakra for success. You do not need to do any of the rituals, but I will let you know that I only have a 100% success rate working with them.

If all of this is a lot, I encourage you to let yourself be exactly where you are, as it is exactly where you are supposed to be. For some of you I will be, and have always been, too much. However, this is not my first rodeo being too much. I am, of course, aware that this may be closing the door for working with some of the people and companies I have supported in the past. And as for the bridges that I may be burning by connecting intuition with business success, I'll tell you—I have a box of matches and we ride at dawn.

Alexandra Phillips is the CEO of Copper Owl Group, an intuitive change management company that works to harness our collective strengths to achieve transformative change. Find out more about her work at CopperOwlGroup.com

Bleak but Marvelous:
The Life of Tatiana Troyanos
by Giselle Sancic

Chapter 1

Tatiana checks her makeup one more time in the lighted mirror on her bedside table. How many times has she done this before, backstage at the Met, the Hamburg Opera, and countless other theaters.

She hums to warm her vocal cords while she adds a touch more rouge to her pale cheeks. She fluffs her thinning dark hair, but nothing can bring back the sparkle in her eyes, now dulled with ache and resignation.

She tries a melody from her role as Octavian in Strauss's *Der Rosenkavalier*. Her mezzo- soprano is still rich, if with less volume. But it would do for today's small gathering.

The high-collared silk blouse she's chosen to wear celebrates the occasion, and hides the frailties of her once statuesque figure. Finally, she puts on her favorite earrings, imitation gold trinkets from her childhood, and her favorite diamond ring, the one she bought for herself with her first singing paycheck. Both are reminders of her meager upbringing and how far she has come.

She leans back in her chair, whispering a phrase from *West Side Story*. It would be nice to include a popular tune if her strength holds up.

A woman enters the room and waits near the door.

"Ready, Miss Troyanos?" she asks.

Tatiana takes her time standing up.

"Yes, thank you."

She wears a blue hospital gown under her frilly blouse. Instead of heels, she wears bedroom slippers. Her balance wavers, and she grips the back of the chair to steady herself.

The nurse steps forward.

"Can I help you?"

"No, I'll be fine."

Tatiana reaches for the IV pole and draws it to her side. She stands as tall as she can, as if she is waiting in the wings for her entrance onto the Metropolitan Opera stage.

"How do I look?" she asks.

"Beautiful, Miss Troyanos. How do you feel?"

Tatiana smiles.

"Today there is no pain."

The nurse opens the door wide and Tatiana steps through, as regal as a queen. She walks down the hallway to the waiting room filled with patients and their families, for her last performance.

#

Back in her hospital bed later that day, on August 21, 1993, Tatiana Troyanos died from cancer. She was 54 years old.

Chapter 2

The name Tatiana means fairy queen, but Tatiana Troyanos' childhood was far from a fairy tale existence. Her difficult early years marked her with insecurities for the rest of her life. "My past is hard to overcome."

Tatiana's father, Nicholas John Troyanos, was born on July 13, 1905, on the Greek island of Cephalonia (Kefalonia). His parents, John and Panayota (née Canalis) Troianos, had four sons; Nicholas was the youngest. The Troianos family lived like most on the island, in a small rural village, eking out an existence by tending to the olive trees and currant shrubs that managed to grow on the steep, rocky hillsides.

But life changed dramatically after the boys' father died when Nicholas was just five years old. Leaving his wife to raise their four sons on her own, they struggled to survive. One-by-one, the brothers immigrated to America in search of work. Nicholas was the last to go. He followed his brothers to New York City in the early 1920s.

The family of Tatiana's mother, Hildegarde née Langerer, also came to America seeking a new beginning. Hildegarde, an only child, was born in Cologne, Germany, on January 1, 1918. World War I raged until November, and the following years proved devastating socially and economically for the German nation. Factories were rebuilt from the rubble, but for the workers toiling in harsh conditions on below-subsistence wages, life could hardly be called livable. The Langerers wanted better for themselves and their daughter. They immigrated first to Canada and then on to New York City in 1930, when Hildegarde was 12 years old.

For the Troyanos and Langerer families, living in New York meant settling into neighborhoods where they could speak their own language, find their own foods in the shops, and celebrate their own customs. Amid the city landscape of many cultures, Nicholas and Hildegard found each other and began a relationship. Opera was the common passion to bring them together. Hildegard, still a teenager, took singing lessons to become a coloratura soprano. Nicholas, while working in the restaurant business, harbored aspirations to be a professional tenor. Tatiana said both her parents had "beautiful voices."

But as their lives became intertwined, their dreams of the stage quickly faded. The couple, not yet married, had their first child, John, on August 12, 1937. Thirteen months later, on September 12, 1938, their daughter Tatiana was born.

After two children, pressure on the couple to marry was intense from both sides of the family. So just two months after Tatiana's birth, they took their vows in a judge's office in downtown Manhattan. Hildegard was 21 years old, and Nicholas was 33. The witnesses at the wedding were the groom's brother, Leo, and his wife, Irene.

But the marriage proved to be a mistake from the very beginning. Differences in background and age were too much to overcome, and neither Nicholas nor Hildegard were ready to take on the responsibilities of caring for two children under the age of two. Tatiana described her mother and father as "ill-matched to each other and ill-suited to parenthood."

The couple separated while Tatiana was still an infant. Hildegard left the home and her children, eventually moving to Florida and getting a divorce. Tatiana would remain estranged from her mother. She always thought of herself as Greek American and seldom acknowledged her German heritage.

Without a wife and with two young children to care for, Tatiana's father, working long hours and far from the fatherly type, came to what seemed the obvious solution. He turned his kids over to his brothers' families to raise.

The Troyanos clan lived in the tenement buildings on the west side of Manhattan (in a prescient coincidence, where the Lincoln Center Metropolitan Opera House now stands). Abandoned by her parents and passed around by the relatives, baby Tatiana grew into a young girl without any sense of herself, much less love. "It was not a normal childhood. I was totally confused, lost and extremely sensitive."

In her despair, she rebelled against her unstable and often neglectful home life. Even her Aunt Irene, the one person she felt close to, could not calm her. Tatiana's angry outbursts became more frequent, and she was finally declared too difficult to deal with. When she was only eight years old, Tatiana was sent away to live at the Brooklyn Home for Children. She would spend the next ten years in institutional care. She never lived with her family again.

The Brooklyn Home, formerly called the Home for Destitute Children, had been relocated to Forest Hills, Queens. Each "cottage" on the site accommodated 20 children, with an adult supervisor. Tatiana was just another lost cause among the many.

Still, she remembered her life at the home as "bleak but marvelous." The marvelous part came during her weekly piano lesson with Mr. Pietrini. Louis Pietrini was a Metropolitan Opera bassoonist who volunteered as a music teacher for the children. He also gave solfège classes to interested youngsters, which Tatiana would later say were the "the basis of my musical education."

Entering her teenage years, however, Tatiana's love of music was not enough to quell her unpredictable and aggressive behavior. Again labeled too difficult to deal with, she was moved to the Girls Service League Home, for "disturbed girls" on East 19th Avenue. Living with other young women given up on by family and society, Tatiana's self-doubt deepened. "I got disturbed. I felt there must be something wrong with me, too."

But Tatiana's piano teacher did not give up on her, or her talent. Mr. Pietrini arranged a piano scholarship for her to the Brooklyn Music School. Offered this lifeline, Tatiana did not waste a minute. She took to her piano studies at the school with enthusiasm and dedication. She also became involved in drama and dance, on the stage and behind the scenes. "I always won the prize for trying the hardest."

While she excelled at the keyboard, her musical aspirations lay elsewhere. "I had a secret desire to sing, and I had a dark sound and was shy, quiet and hardly spoke to anyone. I think I was saving my voice for the years to come."

Tatiana joined the All-City High School Chorus, where a music teacher asked, "who the voice belonged to." Soon after, Tatiana was admitted to the Juilliard Preparatory School. She was 16 years old when she took her first formal voice lesson.

At last she discovered her true self.

Giselle Stancic is a San Francisco Bay Area writer who draws upon her classical music background to give voice to the untold stories of musical performers on and off the stage. Find out more at MusicMysteries.com.

POETRY

Category Winner
Witchery: Do You See Me?
by Shaun Perkins

Do You See Me?

These are the images of myth, the ash smatterings
Swept out the door of your sunny room to form demons
In the air, whipped patterns of smoke-shaped horns,
Smell of sodden leaves and acrid leavings of fire
Long dead in the clearing in the woods you won't enter.

Do you see me?

I'm a stopped page in the book you look at in the corner
Of the library where you can hide it if approached
By others, though you cannot hide being approached
By the other that is the shadow behind the self
Putting on the jeans and t-shirts of everyday living.

Do you see me?

One silent morning, when the cats escaped from the house,
The sky bore down on the pasture as if giving birth,
The pressure in the air like the moment before the pot's lid
Cracked, and the steam found its way out of the cracks
And wrapped tendrils of a dead story around your neck.

Do you see me?

We have walked into a story that someone else devised.
We are searching for a ladder to find our way out.
We are moving just fast enough to keep up with ourselves.
We are turning back the clock in order to make it move.
We are everywhere that everywhere has ever been.

Shaun Perkins is the founder/director of the Rural Oklahoma Museum of Poetry, a teaching artist with the Oklahoma Arts Council, and co-host of the museum podcast Wacky Poem Life. She has published a variety of books and her forthcoming nonfiction one is from Bear Manor Media, *Cocktails, Coquettes and Cigarettes: Perry Mason Concoctions*. Find out more about her at PoemLife.org.

Roadless, Motorless

by Jamie Armstrong

Days before Lewis and Clark saw
waters plunge through a shoreless canyon,
Chief Cameahwait spoke of a river
with banks straight up like a tree—
River of No Return—

Storming into wilderness with rain or snow
or wafting pollen across sunlit meadows
wind passes
uncut wisdom of trees
unmeasured power of water
uplifted joy of mountains.

Humans may enter wilderness
on equal footing with rocks and river rapids
spruce and pine, bears and bighorn sheep.

At night, sky fills with a faint, high-pitched hum
like the sea's sound in a shell. It resonates
throughout the land's dark geography
above forested slopes, in meadows dimly starlit.
Sibilance ever so softly, no tempo.

Wilderness offers an enduring presence,
a primeval source.... Imagine climbing down
your DNA's ladder a thousand generations.
You come to a river near your ancestral village,
which wilderness surrounds. It provides
through nature all that your people will need
to endure for many generations.

As I walk through the paved city
summer warmth rises from sidewalks.
In green pots hanging from lamppost arms,
pansies and daisies wave a little cheer my way.
Cool air arrives from out of town.
Wind brings a wild, wordless message
that moves my spirit with wonder.

Jamie Armstrong writes poems that explore nature—its beauty, processes, and connections to the human spirit. His poems appeared recently in the *A Quiet Wind Speaks, This Gem of a Forest* and the SFWC anthology (2023). Named "Club Poet" by the Mendocino Coast Cyclists, Jamie may be contacted at SteamDonkeyBard@gmail.com.

Invisible

by Robin Gabbert

after Rita Dove's "Daystar"

I seek a palace
among ordinary things,
slip into that space
between dark and light,
among stars and trees.
Find a niche to enter, stay.
My palace, which is not a palace,
is bathed in sunset hues
that soothe, succor, massage,
a moving cloak to protect me.
Sleep is near if needed,
a way out, if desired.

I am not a prisoner here.
But at this moment,
leaving is unfathomable.
There's no need to return
to the creature who snaps and
growls, who finds ways to turn
the simplest things into squabbles.
I'll stay here—
write him into a poem,
paint him into a mural, pick up his
pieces and sew them like animal hides
until they make a pleasing form.

Eventually, I will go back,
back to see the twins, the twins
who are nothing like him.
They—are why I stayed.
Stayed for decades,
even after the meat
started to spoil,
the dessert
no longer appealing.
They're now grown
but I am primeval and

I can always
visit my palace—
the soothing fog between
the dimness and the dusk
because there are those who
do not notice: the shift in the air,
the brief flicker of leaves,
glaze of eyes and ears,
a distant stare, or
the too long
sharpening
of knives

Robin Gabbert has poetry in state, national, and international poetry anthologies including the Ekphrastic Review. Her latest book of poetry is *The Clandestine Life of Paintings, in Poems*. Robin has spoken to the California Writers Club and other groups on Ekphrastic Poetry. She lives in California wine country with her husband Con and pup Hamish where she enjoys good food, wine, and holds a Writers Salon bi-monthly. See RobinGabbert.com.

Capture

by Alissa Larson

I want you
to crack
open
the lid
of the container,
entice me
nearer, one
step nearer,
with sweet
molasses oats.
I want
you to look
into my rolling
eyes and see
my wild. I
want you
to pet my
quivering
body until
it calms.
I want you
to hold
my velvet
muzzle in your
hands, breathe
my fear
away. I
want to lick
the salt off
your hand
as you slide
a soft rope
around
my
neck.

I want to slice the peaches
for you.
I want you

to smell the cinnamon.
I want you
to taste it hot.
I want to make
your bed
with square corners.
I want to plant
dahlias in your
garden. I want
to dust
your piano.
I want to pour
your comfortably
temperate
glass of wine.

Only you
asked me
why I couldn't
make you
a child.
Why
I only
ever tried
to paint you
a poem.

I'll mold a shape for you.

I want to wade
naked in clay
and form vases
vases
vases
vases and
leave them all.
I want to taste
the purple
wildflowers. I want

to run through
twisting
paths up
mountains covered with
wicked
and jagged rocks.
I want to bleed.
I want to really hear
the bird songs,
like they are
the last sound
my dreaming
soul has been
waiting
a lifetime to hear.
I want a hot night
to roar
against the thunder.

A night
that smells of rain and
earth and
dirt and
worms
and earth
until I breathe
only earth.

I'll mold
a shape for
you. You
tamed me
to smithereens.

Alissa Larson is a retired firefighter living in the San Francisco Bay Area. She writes poetry and is working on a memoir that explores social justice issues for female firefighters. Find more of her work at AlissaLarson.com.

Cheapskate Date

by Elizabeth Googe

Champagne and caviar dreams in exchange for
Dungeons and Dragons and Flamin' Hot Cheetos.
We took to the interstate with hopes of two-story homes with pools in the city.
Reality gave us grad school checks and studio ambitions.
-Scratch that
Reality gave us a Covid stipend and discount groceries.
Dumpster diving for furniture.
Quarter soda half off.
Eating dinner on our master degrees and dreaming of going overseas.
Costco wine and hammocks on trees hung in someone's else's backyard.
-until they kick us off.
It's a millennial state of mind with pennies to grind.

I'd rather your face than a crisp dollar bill.
Turn the disillusioned celebrities off our small screen.
Crank up the fan to drown out our neighbor's bass.
Grab the greasy chips and fizzled out coke and let's head to bed.
We've got more wealth between our Wal-Mart sheets
    than those doctorate costs combined.
Here's to the sweatpants and ramen nights.
Cheers to the creatively free dates we've managed.
Capture that inflation and rent in a bottle,
Give me that sultry California sunshine, a relationship
    bred in parks and beaches and sand.
No tax needed, callus fingers hanging loose.

Your Golden Gate, toll dodging hustle is real-
Pandemic tested.
Checkout, please!
My heart is sold.

Elizabeth Googe is a freelance writer and California transplant by way of Mississippi. She writes quirky poetry and fantasy fiction. You can follow her reading and writing journey on Instagram @Dungeons_And_Dragonfruit.

time and space
by Michael Miller

'as there is but one space and one time in
which all forms of phenomena and all
relations of being or not being take place' --kant
it will not last, our lives, all this will pass.
although these days seem solid slipping past
our mortal lives are made of breaking glass.
a forced first breath and into life we're cast
to fill the universe's emptiness
with sorrowed tears, and shouts of sudden joy.
souls spring to life amidst this randomness.
the passing days are counted as a ploy
to make it seem there's something where there's not.
but, then, perhaps the beauty we create,
imposing order on this cosmic knot,
will bring us scenes of awe to celebrate.
　　our senses surf atop time's ebb and flow,
　　construct a life within the space we know.

Michael Miller lives in Edmonds, WA, on the Puget Sound with his wife and their two cats. In 2022, Michael received an honorable mention in the Yeats Society of New York's Poetry Prize and he has twice been a finalist in the SFWC Poetry contest. His poems have appeared in the New Guard Review, Lyric Magazine, The Society of Classical Poets and others. He received his Master's in English from San Francisco State University from the Creative Writing Department.

Catatumbo Symphony

by Daniel Moreschi

As sunset beckons on the mazy, marshy mouth
of Maracaibo Lake, sporadic breezes lead
the water's surface, stirring swirls among the reeds,
creating shimmered mirrors that reflect a shroud

of gray, covertly brimming overhead. Though veiled,
the Andes loom like silent giants, bearing witness
to where tones of wind-kept whispers linger; stillness
fractured by intensified caresses, trailed

from swell-bound blusters. Rustles rattle, ripples race
and flits of wings resound in flurries, just as makeshift herds
of varied species—not knowing where or when to turn—
assail reluctant paths. Their scrambled scansion breaks

with strides aligned; the animals encircle ways,
as if beset by their own shrinking shadows. Amid
the flicker of a dazzling zigzag, steps go still,
then all that can retreat is routed by a wave

of distant thrums: a rat-a-tat of crackling claps
and loops of charge-lit choreographies unite,
as both composer and conductor of the night.
These streaks of sheets unfold in sequences. They wrap

around the clouds in branching arcs. Each flash commands
its own embodied image in the waters. Tempos
alter, lightning extends; crescendos bellow: echoes
of this dance reverberate across the land.

The floors unravel, flora tumbles, trees are traced
along a pass of peaks, while hillsides silhouette.
A dozen hours advance. Between the thunder's threads
and sections, interludes of silence find their place.

The fervor softens, outros pour and lapses grow;
once-restless skies inhale and sigh. As dawn appears,
the marsh is held by restful air; horizons clear
as currents fall and curtains rise to end the show

Daniel Moreschi is a poet from South Wales, UK, who found solace in writing amid his ongoing struggle with severe M.E. He has been acclaimed in over 100 competitions and published in anthologies of prize-winning literature, as well as by *Lunar Codex*, *The Lyric*, *The Sunlight Press*, *Autumn Sky*, *14 Magazine*, *Formal Verse*, *Reach Poetry*, *The Dawntreader*, *Society of Classical Poets*, *WestWard Quarterly*, *The Chained Muse*, *Every Writer Resource*, and many other publications.

Wide Open to Sensation

by Angelica Recierdo

You and I married up and down stony Oporto.
For two euros we walked down the aisle
witnessed by Saint Ildefonso and cashier Hugo.
Our Pagan Catholic vows of gilded suffering
and port-stained poems pouring into the Douro.

I kept my sneakers on in the funicular
while you parted riverbanks,
rollicking at consummate elevation.
We levitate like line-dried bedsheets
waving from the city's most favored balcony.

Your honey pores seep fever and fado.
We do not leave futon country
until gulls are calling for our hearts.

My bootstrapped beloved shaking citrus trees,
I watch your body heave ancient sighs,
my every cell wide open to sensation.

Angelica Recierdo is an MFA candidate in Creative Writing at Dominican University of California and a poetry editor for *The Intima: A Journal of Narrative Medicine*. Her poems are often about navigating the body, relationships, and our shared world. Find her on LinkedIn or Instagram.

Post Loss Tyndall Effect

by Vanessa Shields

he stands in the kitchen   body   not a body   but a hollow

a living ache
    a bag of bones   exhausted under twisted sinew
where is she?   he looks and looks
eyes blurry with anger that he can breathe without her

it's after dinner   when his heart rips again
he doesn't fall to his knees because the kids are moving dishes

around him

    they think he's catching a cold for all the throat issues he's experiencing
blue blue blue sky blue dusk blue midnight blue   death disaster
    all the blues for her   her name stuck in his trachea

the edge of the knife he sharpens coos his wrists
    he hides in the darkened bathroom   suffocating
    a light pushes in   he sees a strand of her golden hair
caught on a mirror nail   it moves in his breath   reaches for him

his face is a wreckage   the sunken aftermath of death's demands

he believes he is dying
    then he remembers the way her nipple rose to meet his mouth

he eats the strand of her hair   swallows swallows swallows

    finally he sobs   spit dazzling his beard   his eyes adjust

senses twitching towards   her   light   it   remains

Vanessa Shields is a poet/writer, teacher, editor living in Windsor, Ontario, Canada. She is the owner of Gertrude's Writing Room, a mobile creative writing school! For all things Vanessa, visit VanessaShields.com or Gertrudes.ca.

El Tapatio

by Paula Wagner

Were you the cute young guy who served me bacon and eggs
at your family's Mexican diner out on Old Highway 99
in southern Oregon that morning so many years ago?
Back when the place was no more than a colorful shack on stilts
long before the arrival of trendy food trucks
or this palatial new restaurant by the same name
You couldn't have been much older than I or more shy
as a teenager on vacation with my family
You kept a poker face to my coy smiles
beneath your mother's eagle eyes
presiding at the cash register
regal as a queen
not missing a thing
Your thick black hair slicked back in a ducktail
Muscles rippling beneath your jeans and tight white T
My red curls unruly as a horse's mane
Your bronze hand sliding the steaming plate
across the checkered oilcloth
mere inches from my galloping heart
Now I can't help noticing how low your silver belt buckle hangs
in this big new space with its glass topped tables and full bar
A testimony to your family's sweat and tears
serving margaritas and fajitas by the bellyful year after year
to gringas like me under the same neon sign
flashing *Bienvenido!* in red and green
When you bring the check I casually comment
that I used to come here as a kid
back at the old location out by the highway
Oh, that was more than thirty years ago
you reply with a distant look in your eye
*but I still see myself working there sometimes
en mis sueños — in my dreams.*

Paula Wagner was born in London, England, and now lives in the San Francisco Bay Area with her husband and two tuxedo cats. Besides writing, she enjoys yoga, swimming, traveling, singing, and the company of her far-flung extended family. She is currently working on a collection of poetry and a sequel to her first memoir, *Newcomers in an Ancient Land* (SheWrites Press, 2019). Paula-Wagner.com

Look for the rest of these stories and more
as our contest winners and finalists grow
their careers through the connections they
make at the San Francisco Writers Conference.

Enter your work next time or join us
at the next class or conference.

SFWriters.org

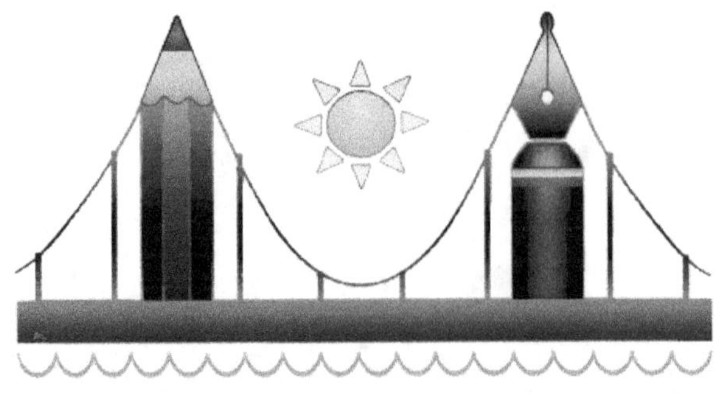

SAN FRANCISCO
WRITERS
CONFERENCE
Learn. Connect. Publish.

New Alexandria
CREATIVE GROUP